Rachael settled onto the swing beside the cowboy.

Pulling her knees to her chest, she wrapped her arms around her legs. "It's chilly."

"Nights are cool this time of year." But Bo's mind wasn't on the temperature, and he wasn't the slightest bit cool. In fact, he'd broken a sweat beneath his denim jacket.

Rachael dropped her gaze to her hands. "You probably know this already, but I'm not very good at following other people's rules. I just tend to be independent."

Independent was an understatement, but Bo didn't say as much. He didn't want to get into the reasons for her recklessness. He didn't like the way he was reacting to her. He didn't want to have to talk to her any longer than necessary. Not because sitting on the porch with her was unpleasant, but because she was making him feel things he didn't want to feel—and tempting him to do things he knew he would regret....

LINDA CASTILLO

OPERATION: MIDNIGHT COWBOY

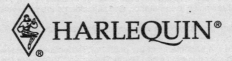

HARLEQUIN®

TORONTO • NEW YORK • LONDON
AMSTERDAM • PARIS • SYDNEY • HAMBURG
STOCKHOLM • ATHENS • TOKYO • MILAN • MADRID
PRAGUE • WARSAW • BUDAPEST • AUCKLAND

ISBN-13: 978-0-373-88737-8
ISBN-10:   0-373-88737-X

OPERATION: MIDNIGHT COWBOY

This edition published by arrangement with Harlequin Books S.A.

® and TM are trademarks of the publisher. Trademarks indicated with ® are registered in the United States Patent and Trademark Office, the Canadian Trade Marks Office and in other countries.

www.eHarlequin.com

Printed in U.S.A.

ABOUT THE AUTHOR

Linda Castillo knew at a very young age that she wanted to be a writer—and penned her first novel at the age of thirteen. She is the winner of numerous writing awards, including the Holt Medallion, the Golden Heart and the Daphne du Maurier Award, and she has been nominated for the prestigious RITA® Award.

Linda loves writing edgy romantic suspense novels that push the envelope and take her readers on a roller-coaster ride of breathtaking romance and thrilling suspense. She resides in Texas with her husband, four lovable dogs and an Appaloosa named George. For a complete list of her books, check out her Web site at www.lindacastillo.com, contact her at books@lindacastillo.com or write her at P.O. Box 577, Bushland, Texas 79012.

Books by Linda Castillo

HARLEQUIN INTRIGUE

CAST OF CHARACTERS

Rachael Armitage—A MIDNIGHT agent on the edge. Two years ago, she shot and killed the son of international crime lord Viktor Karas. Now Karas wants revenge. Can Rachael survive the wrath of one of the most brutal criminals in the world?

Bo Ruskin—After killing a fellow MIDNIGHT agent, he quit the agency and fled to his remote Montana ranch. But the agency needs a favor. Can Bo keep Rachael Armitage safe when he can't even pick up his gun?

Viktor Karas—The most brutal crime lord in the world. Will he succeed in killing the woman responsible for his son's death?

Sean Cutter—He needs a favor from former MIDNIGHT agent Bo Ruskin. Can Cutter count on him to keep Rachael Armitage safe?

Michael Armitage—He was killed in the line of duty six months earlier. But what secrets did Michael take with him to the grave?

Ivan Petrov—The professional killer hired by Viktor Karas. Will he succeed in eliminating his target? Or die trying?

Prologue

They were going to kill her this time.

The first shot blew a hole the size of her thumb through the driver's side window. Rachael Armitage cut the steering wheel hard to the right. The Mustang slid sideways on the rain-slicked road, but she steered into the skid. The instant the tires gripped, she hit the gas.

There was at least one vehicle behind her. Maybe two. The men inside were probably armed to the hilt. The driver was good; he knew when to get close and when to back off. But she was better. She only hoped she had the horsepower to prove it.

Never taking her eyes from the rearview mirror, she negotiated a sharp curve. The car fishtailed, but she held it steady and maintained control. The headlights behind her disappeared. When the road straightened, Rachael floored the accelerator. But she knew they weren't going to give up.

Grabbing her purse, she emptied it onto the seat next to her. For an instant she debated whether to reach for the cell phone or the Beretta .380, but she reached for the phone.

Headlights flashed in her rearview mirror as she flipped open the cell. Cursing, she hit the speed dial with her thumb. The vehicle was gaining on her with astounding speed. Coming too fast. Getting too close. One ring. Two.

"Come on," she snapped.

The vehicle bumped her from behind just as a voice answered. "ID and code, please."

"This is Alpha two-four-six. Code red." Rachael glanced to her left to see a big chrome bumper inches from her window. "Damn."

"What's your twenty, Alpha?"

Knowing the vehicle was going to ram her, Rachael stomped the brake. But she wasn't fast enough. The big SUV swerved, its front quarter panel slamming into the

Mustang hard enough to knock the phone from her hand. The car veered sideways. The tires screamed as they lost purchase.

She skillfully steered into the skid, but her heart was hammering by the time she regained control. Adrenaline burned hot in her gut. *Too damn close,* she thought. These guys were good. Professional killers more than likely. They had heavier, faster vehicles. Bigger guns. But then she didn't expect any less from the man whose only mission in life was to see her dead.

She should have heeded Cutter's advice and taken the Lear. But then Rachael had never been good at taking advice.

Ahead, she could see the yellow glow of Chicago's north suburbs above the tree line. She wasn't familiar with this particular road. Didn't know where to find refuge. Where the hell was a cop when you needed one?

The second shot shattered the windshield. The safety glass held, but shards pelted her like sleet. Large-caliber projectile. High velocity. If they shot through the engine she would be dead in the water.

Wind roared through the hole in the windshield. Cold night air surrounded her with icy fingers. But it wasn't the cold that had her hands shaking on the wheel. A glance at the speedometer told her she was nearing one hundred miles per hour. A dangerous speed even in the best conditions. Downright reckless on wet pavement on a curvy back road in the dead of night.

But then Rachael had always been good at reckless.

Every nerve in her body jumped when two sets of headlights loomed behind her. She pressed the accelerator to the floor, but the Mustang's V-8 engine had already given its all. The second vehicle came up beside her. A large SUV.

The fender slammed into the driver's side door. Steel screeched and groaned as the vehicles locked. Rachael hit the brake, but it was too late. The Mustang careened into the guardrail. Sparks shot high into the air as steel ground against steel. She tried desperately to ease the car back on the road, but the SUV was too heavy. She was going too fast.

In a last-ditch effort to keep the car from going through the guardrail and down the embankment, she jerked the wheel hard to the left. The SUV was ready and slammed into her again. The impact sent the Mustang into a skid. Rachael was thrown violently to the right. The car bounced off the guardrail and went into a wild spin.

She fought the steering wheel for control, but it was a losing battle. She caught a glimpse of headlights. Of trees against the night sky. The lights of Chicago through the white capillaries of the shattered windshield. Vaguely, she was aware of her cell phone and weapon sliding to the floor.

The car spun as if in slow motion. She was thrown against her safety belt when the car hit the guardrail on the opposite side of the road. The splintering of wood sounded like a gunshot. The airbag deployed. Then she was tumbling end over end.

Rachael tried to protect her face and head, but the journey down the embankment was stunningly violent. Even with the airbag in place, her cheek slammed into the steering wheel hard enough to daze her. Glass broke when her temple hit the driver's side window. The car somersaulted like a carnival ride run amok.

After everything she'd been through—every crazy risk she'd taken—she couldn't believe her life would end this way. On some back road in the dead of night at the hands of some faceless, nameless goons she'd never even met. She'd always imagined herself going down in a blaze of glory—and taking at least one of them with her.

She thought of Michael, of all the times in the last two years when she'd wanted nothing more than to lay her head down and join him. She wondered if this was that moment. If the nine lives she'd always fancied herself as having had finally run out. The prospect was not as comforting as she'd imagined.

As suddenly as the car had careened out of control, everything went still. Rachael found herself hanging upside down, suspended by her safety belt. The first thought that registered was that she was alive. She'd had the breath knocked out of her; she could hear herself gasping, trying to get oxygen into her lungs. Her elation was short-lived when the tinny *thunk* of a bullet penetrating steel sounded a foot away from her head. She couldn't believe they were still shooting at her. Time to go.

Mentally, she did a quick physical assessment. A dull throb racked her left shoulder. She was pretty sure the warmth on the left side of her face was blood. But Rachael didn't have time to hurt. She knew the men in the SUV weren't finished. If she wanted to live, she was going to have to drag herself out of the car and make a run for it.

A groan escaped her as she reached for the release on the safety belt. Pain shot from shoulder to elbow, but she didn't let it stop her. Survival took precedence over pain. Mind over matter. She would deal with injuries later.

The belt mechanism clicked open. Gravity slammed her into the steering wheel. Grinding her teeth, she fumbled blindly in the darkness for her cell or weapon. She located the cell on what was left of the dashboard, the Beretta next to the crushed dome light. Shoving both items into the waistband of her jeans, Rachael heaved herself toward the passenger side window.

Tiny shards of glass cut her as she clawed through the small opening. Two more shots rang out as she crawled from the car. The Mustang had landed roof down. Steam hissed from the undercarriage and spewed into the cold night air. A small fire flickered beneath the hood. The car was useless; she was going to have to hoof it.

She scrambled to her feet. An instant of dizziness, then the horizon leveled. Around her, the night showed no signs of the violence that had exploded just seconds earlier. The only sound came from the slow spin of a single wheel and the hiss of steam. A chorus of crickets. The distant bark of a dog.

Voices cut through the silence. Rachael glanced toward the road above her. A fresh surge of adrenaline burned through her when she spotted four men. Illuminated by headlights, they were making their way down the ravine. At least two of them were armed with pistols. The other two carried rifles. In the back of her mind she wondered if they had night-vision equipment.

Persistent sons of bitches, she thought, and launched herself into a lumbering run for the tree line a dozen yards away. Her knee protested, but she didn't slow down.

Shouts rose behind her as she entered

the line of trees. They'd reached the car and discovered her missing. If the situation hadn't been so dire, she might have enjoyed the moment. There was nothing she loved more than besting some piece of scum. But she wasn't out of the woods yet.

Pulling the cell phone from her waistband, she hit the speed dial to the MIDNIGHT Agency's crisis line. The coordinator answered on the first ring. Rachael was breathless when she recited her ID, code and GPS coordinates. The voice told her a chopper team was on the way with an ETA of twenty-five minutes. In that instant, twenty-five minutes seemed like a lifetime. Rachael knew all too well how much could happen in twenty-five minutes.

Shoving the cell phone into her waistband, she prayed she lived long enough to reach the pickup point.

Chapter One

"You want to tell me why I'm here?" Bo Ruskin rubbed a hand over his jaw, aware of the scrape of whiskers that had sprung up on the overnight flight from his ranch outside of Cody, Wyoming, to the small, covert airstrip near Washington, D.C., that was used exclusively by the CIA and its lesser known division, the MIDNIGHT Agency.

He'd received the call just before 11:00 p.m.—a time when more often than not the news wasn't good. He had a sinking feeling Agency Head Sean Cutter was about to prove him right.

"I need a favor," Cutter said.

An alarm went off in Bo's head. He knew all about Sean Cutter and favors.

"Must be a big one for you to ask me to fly here on a moment's notice without so much as an explanation."

Cutter paused outside a tall, mahogany door marked Conference Room and shoved it open. "Have a seat."

Bo barely noticed the glossy wood table or the dozen high-back leather executive chairs surrounding it. He took a seat closest to the door, since he was pretty sure he was going to be using it to make his exit in the next minute or so.

Cutter sat at the head of the table. "One of my operatives needs a safe house and protection."

Bo didn't hesitate. "So follow protocol and put them into witness security."

"I'm sure you're aware that two months ago, Ian Rasmussen hacked the witness security program database. We still haven't recovered, Bo. Eighty percent of our safe house locations were breached. Six high-profile witnesses have been murdered. A dozen cases federal prosecutors have spent years building are down the drain."

"Sounds like you have a problem on your hands."

Cutter's jaw flexed. "I need your help."

"I've been out of the loop for two years. I train horses now, for God's sake. I haven't picked up a rifle since—" Bo bit off the words. "I'm not interested."

"You were a damn good agent, Bo."

"All of your agents are good."

"None of them have a fifteen-hundred-acre ranch in the middle of nowhere."

Realization dawned like cold water being poured down his back. "You want me to hide someone at my ranch."

"It's not in your name, is it?"

Nothing he owned was in his name. One of the prices a former agent had to pay. But if Bo Ruskin was anything, he was cautious. He'd learned that the hard way. "I formed a corporation after I left the agency. Everything is registered under the Dripping Springs Cattle Company."

Cutter nodded. "I wouldn't ask just anyone, Bo. There are risks involved. High risks. You're one of the most capable men I know."

"Risks like what?"

"She's got a contract on her head."

"A contract?" he repeated dumbly.

"Well, two, actually."

"Sounds like a trouble magnet."

"Let's just say she's not afraid to jump into the thick of things."

"Cutter, I'm sure you have a contingency plan for these kinds of situations."

"You are my contingency plan."

Bo muttered a curse. "So what did she do? Who did she tick off?"

Cutter leaned forward, as if even within the secure walls of the MIDNIGHT Agency headquarters, someone might hear what he was about to say. "She shot and killed Viktor Karas's son."

The words echoed like the retort of a killing shot. For an instant the only sound came from the hum of heat running through the vents in the ceiling.

"Karas wants her dead," Cutter said. "I don't have to tell you what that son of a bitch is capable of."

Just hearing the name was enough to make the hairs on Bo's neck prickle. Viktor Karas ran one of the most brutal crime syndicates in the world. Arms. Drugs. Prostitution. The last Bo had heard, the kingpin was working on getting a nuke for some terrorist group.

"It was self-defense," Cutter added. "Her cover was blown during a sting. All

hell broke loose. There was a firefight."
He shrugged. "Nikolai Karas took one in
the head."

Bo felt no sympathy. Viktor Karas's brutality and penchant for violence knew no
bounds. He'd taken out more than one good
man over the years. Whoever took on the
responsibility of protecting this woman
would be placing himself and everyone he
knew in danger.

"Karas has pretty much declared war
on the MIDNIGHT Agency," Cutter continued.

"You got yourself covered?"

"We've got the best security in the
world." He shrugged. "Every employee all
the way down to the cleaning crew has a
high-security clearance. I'm not worried
about the agency. I am, however, worried
about this operative."

"So who is it?" Bo asked.

"You've met her."

Bo waited, knowing deep in his gut that
he was about to get hit with another curve.

"Rachael Armitage," Cutter said.

Armitage.

The name struck him with the force of a
dagger plunging into his solar plexus. Two

years ago Michael Armitage had been Bo's best friend. They'd gone through the police academy together. Been cops on the mean streets of Washington, D.C., together. They'd joined the MIDNIGHT Agency together. Worked undercover, choreographing and executing some of the most complex and dangerous stings in the agency's history. Then Michael had been killed. His wife became a widow at the age of twenty-seven. And Bo had given up the only career he'd ever known.

"I'm not interested," Bo heard himself say.

"Look, I know you and Mike were friends."

"We were more than friends. Damn it, you know what happened."

"I know none of it was your fault."

For the first time in a long time, Bo wanted to run. God knew he was good at it. He wanted out of that conference room. Away from Sean Cutter's discerning gaze. He wanted to run back to Wyoming to his ranch and horses. It was the only place in the world where he could breathe. Where he didn't have to think about what had gone down two years ago...

"If I can't convince you," Cutter said, "maybe this will."

Bo's heart was pounding as he watched Cutter open a thin manila folder and shove several photos toward him. "This is what Karas does to the people who cross him."

Bo didn't want to look, but he did, just as Cutter knew he would. He saw horrific images that disturbed him a hell of a lot more than he wanted to admit. "You always were a manipulative bastard."

Cutter didn't even try to look contrite. "I still am."

"Yeah, well, this time it isn't going to work." Bo stood so abruptly, his chair fell over backward. He was midway to the door when Cutter stopped him by grabbing his arm.

"She's in danger, Bo. There have been two attempts on her life in the last week. Karas nearly got her last time. She's on the edge. She's been that way since Michael died. She won't admit it, but she's running scared." He grimaced. "For God's sake, she's been through enough."

"We all have," Bo snapped.

Cutter's eyes flashed. "You owe me, damn it."

Bo jerked his arm from Cutter's grasp, then jabbed a shaking finger in the other man's face. "Don't go there, Cutter. Don't try to use my friendship to manipulate me into doing something I do not want to do."

"Or something you're afraid to do." Cutter's eyes burned into Bo's. "Maybe you're not the man for the job after all. Maybe you're not the man I thought you were."

The words rankled, but Bo didn't let himself react. The urge to walk out that door and never look back tugged at him like a powerful tide. But while Sean Cutter might be manipulative, what he'd said was true. Bo did, indeed, owe him. More than he could ever repay in his lifetime.

Shaking his head, Cutter stalked to the door and yanked it open. His hard eyes landed on Bo. "Go ahead. Run. Run back to Wyoming like you did two years ago."

Aware that he was sweating beneath his leather jacket, Bo usurped the knob from the other man and closed the door. "How long?" he heard himself ask.

"A few days." Cutter shrugged. "A couple of weeks max. Long enough for us to dig up something on Karas that will keep the federal prosecutors happy."

"You already have charges on him."

"Prosecutors want to go for the gold. The big stuff that will keep him behind bars for a long time. Once he's in custody, you're off the hook."

If Bo hadn't felt so lousy about the entire situation, he might have laughed at Cutter's choice of words. When it came to Rachael Armitage, Bo would never be off the hook.

RACHAEL SWORE she wouldn't let them see her sweat. In the past that personal vow had always been enough to keep her cool—at least on the outside—through even the toughest ordeals. But as she made her way down the marble-tiled hall of the MIDNIGHT Agency headquarters toward the conference room, the silk blouse beneath her jacket clung to her back. The briefing she was about to attend wasn't going to be pleasant. The only question that remained was just how bad it was going to be. Sean Cutter had a reputation for being tough.

Yeah, well, so did she.

She did her utmost not to limp as she entered the conference room. Gritting her teeth against the pain in her knee, she squared her shoulders and walked with as much grace as she could muster to the high-back executive chair. She was acutely aware of the two men present watching her, but she didn't acknowledge them. The last thing she wanted was for them to see the nerves zinging just below the surface.

Sean Cutter sat at the head of the table, studying a brown expanding file. Her file, she was sure. A file that was a little too thick, the documents inside a little too worn from too many fingers paging through them too many times. Such had been the nature of her career with the MIDNIGHT Agency.

The sight of the second man gave her pause. She'd seen him before. Met him at some point. But for the life of her she couldn't remember his name. She couldn't remember where she'd seen his face. Odd, because his was a memorable face. Dark eyes. Hawkish nose. Square jaw that hadn't been shaved for at least twenty-four hours. His body language and the directness of his stare told her he was law enforcement. The jeans and cowboy boots told her he held disdain for any kind of dress code. Who was he and what the hell was he doing here?

She looked at Cutter and frowned. "You wanted to see me?"

He frowned back, watching her the way a disapproving parent might watch an unruly teenager who was about to be grounded for life. "Have a seat."

Never taking her eyes from her superior, she sat opposite the cowboy and set her leather pad on the table in front of her.

"How are you feeling?" Cutter asked.

"Good enough to return to work." She gazed at him levelly. "I'm hoping you won't disappoint me."

The two men exchanged a look she didn't understand. A look that gave her a bad feeling in the pit of her stomach. "It looks a lot worse than it is," she said, referring to the bruises on her face.

"I have the report from the doc right here." Cutter looked down at the file. "Dislocated shoulder. The laceration on your left temple required seven stitches. You had fluid drained from your knee." He scowled at her. "I guess it sounds worse than what it really is, too, huh?"

Rachael flushed. "I heal fast."

"Yeah, and I wasn't born yesterday."

It was then that she knew the minor injuries she'd sustained in the car crash were the least of her worries. "I can do desk work until the bruises fade."

"No need because effective immediately you are on administrative leave."

An emotion that was alarmingly close to panic gripped her and squeezed. "Cutter, I feel fine."

"This isn't about how you feel."

"With all due respect, sir, I feel I would be much more effective in the field. You know that."

"What I know is that the most powerful crime lord in the world wants you dead. It's my responsibility to make sure he doesn't succeed."

"But—"

"This is Bo Ruskin," he interrupted, nodding at the cowboy.

Ruskin.

Her memory stirred. Ruskin was a former MIDNIGHT agent. He and Michael had worked together. They'd been friends.

Ruskin had been there the night Michael was killed....

"We've met," she said. *At the funeral.* No wonder she hadn't remembered him. Those dark weeks following her late husband's death had been a blur of grief and rage and insurmountable loss....

"Yes, ma'am," Ruskin drawled in a deep baritone.

Cutter continued. "You will be accompanying Agent Ruskin to an undisclosed location this afternoon for safekeeping until Karas is apprehended."

The words jerked her back to the matter at hand. "I'm afraid that's not possible," she said.

"I'm afraid that's an order," Cutter returned.

"You can't take me off Karas now." She held her fingers a fraction of an inch apart. "I'm this close to nailing him."

"And he came that close to killing you three days ago." Cutter sighed, then looked at Bo Ruskin. "Can you excuse us a moment?"

"You bet." The cowboy rose, tipped his hat at her, then started toward the door.

Rachael got the impression of wide

shoulders, narrow hips encased in denim and cowboy boots. But her focus was on the man yanking the proverbial rug out from beneath her feet.

"Cutter, please don't do this," she said, hating the pleading tone of her voice. "I'm close to—"

"You have twenty minutes to gather your notes and files on Karas and turn everything over to me."

She almost couldn't believe her ears. "You're assigning my case to another team?"

"Not that you've ever been much of a team player. But yes, I'm assigning a fresh team."

"That's incredibly unfair."

"This is not about fair. It's about keeping you alive. Keeping you healthy." Cutter leaned forward. His eyes sought hers, held them. "You're a good agent, Rachael. One of my best. I don't want to lose you. But you need some downtime. I advise you to make the best of this." He motioned toward her shoulder. "Get yourself healed. Get your perspective back. The last couple of years have been tough for you."

"I've dealt with it," she ground out, hating that her voice quivered.

"You can't even say it."

"I've dealt with Michael's death, damn it. I have."

"You've dealt with it by working yourself into the ground. By jumping first and thinking later. I should have put a stop to it long before now."

"I shouldn't be penalized for not being afraid to do my job."

"I'm not penalizing you. But in case you haven't figured it out by now, good old-fashioned fear is what keeps us alive. It's what keeps us healthy in our line of work. And you don't seem to have it anymore."

"I don't have a death wish, if that's what you're imply—"

He raised his hand and cut her off. "You are to treat your leave as you would any covert operation. No one knows where you are. Business as usual. You got that?"

"I don't agree with what you're doing."

"Duly noted." Cutter looked at his watch. "Let's find Ruskin."

BO'S LEGS WERE SHAKING by the time he reached the lobby. He wanted to chalk it up to a sleepless night and the long flight from Wyoming. But he knew the queasy stomach and muscles knotted like ropes between his shoulder blades had nothing to do with fatigue—and everything to do with a woman whose face he still saw in his dreams.

In the years he and Michael had worked together, he'd caught glimpses of her. From photos mostly, since Mike had always tried to keep his personal life as far removed from work as possible. She was a tawny-haired beauty with green eyes and the kind of smile that could bring a man to his knees. He'd listened to Michael speak of her, and Bo had been envious. On more than one occasion, Bo had razzed his fellow agent about how lucky he was to be married to the most beautiful woman in the world.

It wasn't too far from the truth.

Rachael Armitage was even more beautiful now than he remembered. Tougher. A little rough around the edges. But then that's what happened to people in this line of work.

Bo ought to know.

The one and only time he'd met her was

at the funeral. She'd been somehow softer back then. Not quite so thin. He remembered the way the black dress she'd worn had contrasted starkly against her pale complexion. She'd looked fragile and grief-stricken and…shattered.

But then Michael Armitage's death had shattered a lot of people.

Standing at the bank of windows, looking out at the dreary day beyond, Bo thought he could still smell her. A warm, female scent that reminded him of mountain columbine and rain. Wild and fragile and recklessly beautiful. Just like her.

"Bo."

Cutter's voice drilled into his thoughts. Bo spun to find the agency head and Rachael standing a few feet away. "Did you file the flight plan?" Cutter asked.

Bo nodded. "We take off in forty-five minutes."

"Good." Cutter turned to Rachael, assessed her the way a coach might assess an injured high school athlete. One that was good, but had to quit the season due to an injury. "I'm the only person who knows where you're going. No one at the agency has a clue. Keep it that way."

"Yes, sir." But she didn't look happy about any of what was happening. Bo wasn't happy about it, either. But for the first time since he'd walked away from the agency, he was duty-bound to do the right thing.

"I don't expect anything to go wrong," Cutter said. "If it does, initiate a code ninety-nine."

"Roger that," Bo said, falling easily into the old jargon.

"I'd like you to keep me posted on Karas," Rachael said.

Cutter shook his head. "You will have no communication with the agency, unless, of course, you're in danger or need help. He's pretty much declared war on the agency. You know how sophisticated Karas's organization is. Last we heard he had access to a satellite."

She uttered an unladylike curse that left no room for doubt with regard to how she felt about all of this. Had the circumstances been different, Bo might have smiled. Rachael Armitage was a woman to be reckoned with. But she was also Michael's widow. A woman whose life he himself had played a role in devastating. A woman who would have every right to hate him if she knew the truth.

It was up to him to make sure she never did.

"WHY IS RACHAEL Armitage still alive?"

Viktor Karas's cultured voice reverberated through the elegant confines of his study. In his prime at the age of fifty, he was distinguished-looking with tastefully coifed salt-and-pepper hair and eyes the color of a Siberian lake.

Those cold gray eyes landed on one of the two men sitting in tapestry wingback chairs adjacent his desk. Vladimir Novak was young and cocky. But his eyes were ancient. They were the eyes of a killer. And it was precisely the reason Karas had hired him.

Vladimir squirmed. "She escaped."

"Escaped?"

"We tracked her to Chicago. Caught up with her on a back road. We forced her off the road."

"And she got away," Karas finished.

"H-her car rolled down an embankment. By the time we reached it, she'd fled on foot. We pursued her, but it was dark. The terrain was difficult."

Despite his hatred for the woman—the federal agent who'd murdered his beloved Nikolai—Karas felt a fleeting moment of respect for her. Only the most talented and brutal men worked for him. It would take daring, resourcefulness and a good bit of luck to elude them. Rachael Armitage appeared to possess generous amounts of all three traits.

"Twice you have attempted to kill her," Karas said. "Twice you have failed."

"I am sorry," Vladimir said. "But she appears to be well-trained."

Crossing to the wet bar adjacent to a row of windows that offered a stunning view of Moscow's Teatralnaya Square, Karas snagged three crystal tumblers and poured two fingers of vodka into each. He handed tumblers to the two men.

"My son has been dead for a month now and you are no closer to completing your mission than when you started."

"We have listening devices in place." The second man spoke for the first time. "We're working on finding a weak point at the MIDNIGHT Agency."

Karas turned his attention to Ivan Petrov and smiled inwardly. He was also young—not yet twenty-five—and sported a goatee and ponytail that reached halfway down his back. He might look like some pampered New York model, but in the two years he'd been with the organization, Ivan had exterminated more men than the sum of his years.

Karas refocused his attention on the first man. After all, it was Vladimir who had been in charge of both missions. It was Vladimir who had failed. Failure was the one thing Viktor Karas would not tolerate.

"How do you plan to rectify the situation?" Karas asked.

Made nervous by his superior's scrutiny, Vladimir lifted the tumbler and drank, his eyes looking anywhere but into the cold depths of his employer's gaze. "I am flying to the United States first thing in the morning. I'm meeting my contact in New York. I'm hoping he will have information for me with regard to the woman's location."

"You're certain this contact has information for you?"

"This contact—a former agent with the American CIA—has always come through for me in the past. I have information that would destroy him if it were to get back to his superiors."

"I see." Viktor ran his finger around the rim of the glass. "And then?"

"I will find her and kill her." Looking pleased with himself, Vladimir cleared his throat.

Karas contemplated him coldly. "This is your great plan?"

Vladimir put his hand to his mouth and coughed. He sipped the vodka as if to clear his throat, but the coughing worsened. His face reddened. Noticeably uncomfortable, he shifted in the chair. The coughing turned into choking. Sweat broke out on his forehead. Placing both hands to his throat, he made a strangled sound and twisted in the chair.

"Помогите, пожалуйста." *Please, help.*

Karas sipped his vodka, unmoving.

Vladimir's coughing turned violent. White foam spewed from his lips. Eyes bulging, he reached for Karas, but the older man stepped back, out of reach. "You," he croaked.

Karas smiled at him dispassionately. "Yes," he said. "Me. Have a nice trip to hell."

Vladimir clawed at his throat. Throwing his head back, he twisted and fell from the chair. He writhed on the Persian carpet, clutching his throat and gurgling unintelligibly in Russian. After a few minutes, his eyes rolled back white. A final gasp and he lay still.

For several seconds the only sound came from the traffic along the boulevard two stories down. Then Karas walked to the bar and refilled his tumbler. "A new poison my chemist developed," he said. "Most expeditious, don't you agree?"

Ivan Petrov's Adam's apple bobbed twice in quick succession. "Yes," he said, looking down at his own glass of vodka.

Karas threw his head back and laughed. "Go ahead. Enjoy your vodka. You needn't worry that I've poisoned you."

But the younger man's hand trembled when he raised the glass to his lips. "Wh-why did you poison Vladimir?"

"Because he failed. It is the one thing I will not tolerate." Crossing to the young man in the chair, Karas put his hand on the other man's shoulder and squeezed. "Do you understand?"

"Perfectly, Mr. Karas."

"You will find the American agent. You will leave Moscow today. My private jet is waiting. When you find her, you will contact me immediately. I will take it from there. Am I clear?"

"Crystal," the young man replied and downed his remaining vodka in a single gulp.

Chapter Two

The Dripping Springs Ranch was exactly the kind of place where Rachael would never venture. A born-and-bred city girl, she much preferred the excitement of city lights. The ranch was about as far away from city lights as a person could get without leaving the planet.

But as the SUV bounced down a dirt road on a ridge overlooking a valley, she had to admit the high plains and mountains of northwestern Wyoming possessed a stark beauty she would never find in New York. Of course that wasn't going to make sitting on the sidelines any easier.

The thought of being stuck out in the middle of nowhere while another team worked *her* case filled her with frustration—and a terrible sense of being out of the loop. Rachael had wanted to be the one to nail Viktor Karas. As far as she was concerned Sean Cutter owed her that. After all, Karas was indirectly responsible for her late husband's death. She'd spent the last two years working to nab him; she'd worked hard and built a strong case. It rankled that she'd been forced to turn months of effort over to someone else.

"You ever been to a working ranch before?" Bo Ruskin's slow drawl tugged her from her reverie.

Rachael frowned at him, annoyed because he wasn't as miserable as she was. He was wearing a cowboy hat and a denim jacket. He looked comfortable behind the wheel of the truck. As if he didn't have a care in the world.

"Never had a desire to," she replied in a clipped tone.

"Not enough bad guys for you?"

"Something like that."

He sighed. "Look, I know you don't want to be here any more than I want you here, but since Cutter is evidently holding all the cards, we're going to have to get through this."

It was the understatement of the year, especially the part about her not wanting to be there. But Rachael couldn't think of how to change the situation. Without losing her job, anyway.

Raising her hand, she displayed a small gap between her thumb and forefinger. "I was this close to nailing Karas."

"From what I hear, Karas came that close to killing you."

"I got into a scrape," she conceded. "But what agent hasn't over the years? Cutter overreacted."

Bo Ruskin looked away from his driving, his expression telling her he wasn't impressed by her wrath—and that he didn't necessarily agree with her.

Their vehicle passed beneath a steel pipe arch bearing a sign that read Dripping Springs Ranch. Beyond, a white clapboard house and several outbuildings stood prettily against an endless blue sky. Within the confines of a neat pipe fence, several spotted horses looked up from their grazing.

"So what do you do out here?" Rachael asked, taking in the barns and fenced corrals.

One side of his mouth curved. "You mean out here in the middle of nowhere?"

"Well...yeah."

"I train and breed horses, mostly." He parked in front of the garage and killed the engine. "Run fences. Repair the outbuildings when the wind kicks up."

"Seems...quiet."

"It is."

"Do you ever miss being an agent?"

His eyes darkened for a fraction of a second. "Nope."

A man of few words, she thought. Probably a good thing at this point because she didn't feel much like talking. She wasn't sure she'd like what he had to say, anyway. Maybe they'd get along after all.

Or maybe not.

He hefted her single suitcase from the back and carried it to the front door of the house. Rachael had never been a fan of anything country, but the house made a lovely picture against the backdrop of crisp blue sky and purple-hued mountains. A railed porch wrapped around the front of the house. Geraniums grew in profusion from an old wooden barrel that had been split in half and filled with soil. A dinner bell dangled from a hook just outside the door. Beyond, an old-fashioned porch swing rocked in the breeze.

The screen door squeaked when he opened it. Rachael stepped into a large, open living room adorned with rustic furniture and lots of rough-hewn wood beams. A Native American rug graced a pine floor. Beyond was a small but well-appointed kitchen and a window that offered a stunning view of the mountains.

"That's Bareback Mountain."

"It's lovely."

"You've got the guestroom upstairs."

Rachael followed him up the staircase to a narrow hall with five doors. They passed three bedrooms and a large bathroom equipped with an antique claw-footed tub.

The fourth bedroom was small but comfortable with terra-cotta paint, fresh white wainscoting and an intricately made quilt on the twin-size bed. A feminine touch graced the room and she found herself wondering about his decorator. "This is nice," she said.

"Pauline cooks and cleans a couple of times a week. I let her furnish the room about a year ago."

"She did a good job." She wondered about his relationship with Pauline.

He looked large and out of place in the small room, like a wild animal that was trapped indoors.

"I make tortillas and tamales for dinner, *Señor* Ruskin," came a female voice from the hall.

Rachael spun to find a small, dark-eyed woman at the door. She wore a full skirt, denim vest—and cowboy boots. Her eyes widened when they landed on Rachael. "Hello."

Bo cleared his throat. "Pauline, this is Rachael Armitage." His gaze flicked to Rachael. "Pauline Ortegon runs the house and just about everything else here at Dripping Springs."

"Nice to meet you," Rachael said.

The woman was fiftyish with long black hair shot with silver and pulled into a ponytail that reached all the way to the waistband of her skirt. Turquoise earrings in the shape of horses dangled from her lobes. The only thing missing, Rachael thought, was the gun belt and six-shooter.

"Welcome to Dripping Springs Ranch," Pauline said with a strong Spanish accent.

"Rachael's going to be staying with us a few days," Bo said.

"Oh." The woman's eyebrows lifted in surprise. Questions flitted in her eyes, but she did not voice them. "In that case, I will bring clean linens and soaps." She started toward the door, but turned before going through it. "I make tamales and tortillas for tonight for supper."

"Thank you," Bo said.

Nodding, she left the room.

Rachael looked down at the small bed, wishing she was anywhere but here. "I didn't mean to sound ungrateful about staying here," she said. "I appreciate your putting me up."

"I owe Cutter a favor." His smile looked more like a grimace. "This ought to even things up."

A shadow passed over his eyes at the mention of the favor. Rachael wondered what the debt was. "You must owe him big time, since you're no longer an agent."

"Cutter and I go way back. He wouldn't have asked if he wasn't seriously worried about your safety." He motioned toward the window and the ranch spread out beyond. "He knew the ranch would be the perfect place for you to lay low."

"Laying low isn't my style," she muttered.

"It is while you're here."

A sharp retort hovered on her tongue, but Rachael didn't voice it. Her beef was with Cutter, not Bo Ruskin. Still, the idea of spending the next week stuck in this room disheartened her. "So how do you spend your days here?"

"Work mostly."

She tried again. "What kind of work?"

"I train horses. For area ranchers. Breeders. People who show them."

She remembered seeing the horses grazing in the pasture when they'd driven up the lane to the house. "Spotted horses?"

"Appaloosas." Looking anxious to leave, he shoved his hands into the pockets of his snug, faded jeans. "Do you know how to ride? There are some pretty trails on the ranch."

She laughed, but it was a nervous sound. She didn't like the fish-out-of-water sensation creeping over her. "I rode a couple of times when I was a teenager. I'm not very good at it."

"I have a gentle mount if you want to do some exploring."

She hadn't ridden since she was thirteen, to be exact, and spent most of that day on her rump. "Do you have a mode of transportation that doesn't entail hooves?"

One side of his mouth curved into a half smile. "A four-wheeler."

"Now you're talking."

"If you want to take a spin, just let me or Pauline know. I'll leave a map of the ranch on the counter for you."

"Thank you."

"I also have a ranch foreman. Jimmy Hargrove. He's a little crusty, but if you need anything he'll be happy to help you."

Rachael studied him for a moment, her mind taking her back to the one and only time she'd met him. Michael's funeral. She'd been so grief-stricken that day, she barely remembered. But she did remember Bo Ruskin's eyes. When he'd approached her and offered his hand in sympathy for her loss, his gaze had reflected the same devastation she'd felt in her own heart. And at that moment, she'd known he was grieving, too.

"We've met once before," she said.

"I remember." His jaw flexed. "Mike's funeral."

She didn't let herself think of those dark days often. But she found herself curious about this man's relationship with her late husband. "He always spoke fondly of you," she said.

His expression darkened. As if someone had flipped a switch inside him, she felt him closing himself off from her. Erecting a wall. "I've got to get to work." Turning, he started toward the door. "If you need anything let me know."

"How about a flight back to civilization?" she called out.

BY 4:00 P.M. Rachael was bouncing off the walls. She was accustomed to long work days filled with adrenaline. She was used to getting by on four or five hours of sleep for nights on end. She routinely participated in undercover operations where the heady rush of danger was the rule, not the exception.

The Dripping Springs Ranch offered none of that.

After an hour of quiet and birdsong, Rachael had had enough.

Deciding it wasn't too late to make the best of a day that had already been mostly wasted, she slipped into a pair of jeans, a sweatshirt and sneakers. Throwing a jacket and her Beretta .380 into her backpack, she headed downstairs.

She found Pauline in the kitchen, stirring a steaming pot of something spicy and savory. "It smells wonderful," she said.

The dark-haired woman turned and gave her an assessing look. "Tamales," she said in a perfect Spanish pronunciation.

Rachael slid onto a stool at the bar. "So how long have you worked for Bo?"

"Two years now. Since he buy the ranch."

So he'd bought the ranch at about the same time Michael had died. She wondered if his former partner's death had anything to do with it.

Pauline arched an eyebrow. "Are you going somewhere?"

"I thought I'd do some exploring. Bo said he would leave a map of the ranch for me."

"I have it right here." Wiping her hands

on her apron, Pauline went to a small built-in desk and pulled a single sheet of paper from its surface. "Are you going to ride Lily?"

Rachael assumed she was referring to the gentle horse Bo had told her about. "I thought I might take the four-wheeler out for a while."

"Ah." Pauline crossed to the refrigerator and pulled out two bottles of water. "Take these."

"Thank you." Rachael dropped the bottles into her backpack.

Pauline went back to the stove. "Supper is served at six o'clock sharp."

Her stomach rumbling, Rachael took another long whiff of the air. "Believe me, I won't be late."

She let herself out the back door. The air was crisp, but the sun warmed her back as she took the cobblestone walk to the barn. The earthy smells of horses and hay met her when she entered. She was midway down the aisle when a commotion just outside the rear door caught her attention.

Several yards from the barn, Bo Ruskin stood in a steel, round pen with a beautiful young horse. On the end of a long rope, the horse was obviously frightened, snorting and throwing its pretty head high into the air. Dust billowed as horse and man danced on the sandy ground.

Rachael approached the round pen slowly so she wouldn't scare the animal. She watched, mesmerized, as the horse reared, flailing its front hooves at Bo. But the cowboy stayed a safe distance away and held the rope secure. All the while, he talked to the frightened animal in a calm, lulling tone.

"Easy, boy," he cooed. "Come on now. You can do it."

Sweat stained the back of his shirt between his shoulder blades. Dust coated his jeans from the knees down. The horse galloped in a circle around him on the end of the rope, tugging violently. But Bo remained calm, never losing patience with the animal, his tone never altering.

"Settle down," he whispered. "You know I'm not going to hurt you."

Rachael had never been unduly interested in horses—just a short phase in her preteen years—but watching the lanky cowboy work the animal, she felt something unfamiliar and vaguely uncomfortable stir inside her. A feeling she didn't want to acknowledge. A yearning she thought she'd never feel again in her lifetime.

Appalled by the realization that she was more mesmerized by the man than the horse, she stepped back into the barn and pressed her back against the stall door. What the hell was she thinking? Bo Ruskin had been her husband's friend. He'd been there the night Michael had died. How could she feel anything for any male when only two short years had passed since her husband's death?

A hard and ugly guilt churned in her stomach. The logical side of her brain told her the return of her hormones was a normal thing. After all, Rachael hadn't yet seen her thirtieth birthday; her life was far from over.

But the emotional part of her psyche— the part of her that was still a mourning widow—berated that part of her for betraying the husband she'd loved and lost.

"You look like you've just seen a ghost."

Rachael jolted at the sound of Bo's voice and spun to see him standing just inside the barn door. Silhouetted by the sun, his image bestowed the impression with a tough, athletic build born of hard and physical labor. He wore a large silver-and-gold buckle and a leather belt adorned with an intricate design. Lower, she caught a glimpse of a part of his anatomy she did not want to think about.

"I won it in a rodeo down in Cody last year."

Rachael's gaze snapped to his. "What?"

"The belt buckle."

"Oh." A hot blush heated her cheeks. "How did you win it?"

"I rode a bull by the name of Bone Cruncher. Made the eight seconds, but I broke my leg on the dismount."

"Sounds like the bull lived up to his name."

He grinned. "Yeah, but I got the buckle."

"It's...nice." But Rachael didn't dare look at the buckle in question. It was to close to...something else she did not want to see.

The hat he wore shadowed his eyes, but she knew they were on her. Probably wondering why she was acting like such an idiot.

"I—I didn't mean to disturb your work," she blurted when she could no longer stand the awkward silence.

"I reckon both of us have had just about had enough for the day."

She blinked.

"The horse." Amusement danced in his eyes for an instant, then he looked over his shoulder toward the round pen where another man was walking the horse. "I'd like to use him as a stud, but if he keeps up that attitude I might have to geld him."

Rachael knew it was a silly reaction—animals were neutered all the time—but she blushed. "He's beautiful."

"He's a handful, that's for sure. Doesn't like to be told what to do."

"I know the feeling," she muttered.

He laughed outright. "I bet you do." His gaze landed on the backpack she held at her side. "Running away from home already?"

"I was thinking about borrowing your four-wheeler and doing some exploring."

"Did you get a map from Pauline?"

She patted the bag. "Along with some water and a few tortillas."

"She makes the best tortillas in the

world." He motioned toward a small outbuilding a few yards from the barn. "I'll
show you how to fire up the ATV. You're
welcome to it anytime."

He started toward the shed. Rachael fell
in beside him, silently berating herself for
acting like some silly school girl. Bo
Ruskin wasn't the first attractive man she'd
ever dealt with. Unfortunately, he was the
only man in the last two years that had
caused her to go totally brain-dead.

They reached the shed, and he opened
the door. A large four-wheel ATV sat
inside. Wordlessly, he slid onto the seat
and turned the ignition key. The engine
started on the first try.

"Helmet is over there," he said, motion-
ing to one of two helmets hanging neatly
on the wall. "Red one will probably fit you
best."

Rachael picked up the red helmet. When
she turned around, he'd already eased the
vehicle forward and out of the shed.
Leaving the engine running, he slid off
the seat and motioned for her to get on.
"You ever driven one of these things
before?"

"No, but I'm mechanically inclined."

Sliding the helmet onto her head, she climbed onto the seat. "And I have a level four drive rating," she added. Level five was the highest rating.

"I'm impressed, but you still get a lesson."

Resisting the urge to roll her eyes, she nodded.

Bo set his finger against the right handlebar grip. "You have your gas here on the left. Brake on the right."

"I'll try to remember that."

Surprise rippled through her when he bent to fasten the chinstrap. His eyes met hers through the Plexiglas shield. They were the same endless blue as the Wyoming sky. "You sure you can handle this thing?" he asked.

"You tell me." Tired of being underestimated, Rachael revved the engine and let off the brake.

Bo stepped back just in time to avoid being run over.

Spewing gravel, the ATV leapt forward like a big mechanical beast. Gripping the seat with her thighs, Rachael swung the vehicle into a 360-degree circle.

Bo stood near the shed, watching her and

shaking his head. "You're pretty sure of yourself, aren't you?"

"I've been accused of that once or twice."

"Don't go too far. And be careful once you get on the trail. A lot of country out there."

"I think I can handle it." She patted the purring engine.

"I was talking about the cougars and black bears," he said deadpan.

The mention of fanged carnivores gave her pause. Rachael might be a whiz at taking down someone twice her size armed with a gun, but the thought of facing down an animal with claws and teeth made her rethink the wisdom of her afternoon jaunt to the trails. "They'll have to catch me first."

Without waiting for a reply, she hit the gas and headed toward the ridge on the north side of the ranch.

THE DIRT TRAIL was well-marked and ran north for several miles before curving south and looping back toward the ranch. At the top of the northernmost ridge, the land fell away into a postcard-pretty valley where horses and cattle grazed on golden prairie grass.

Rachael stopped the ATV at a good vantage point and shut down the engine. Removing her helmet, she shook out her hair and just sat there staring at the scene. Around her, a light breeze whispered through the tops of the tall ponderosa pines and low-growing juniper. Birds twittered and swooped in the branches. Somewhere in the distance a cow bawled for her calf.

Pulling the water bottle from her backpack, Rachael drank deeply, savoring every cold swallow. Alone and surrounded by nature, her every sense seemed heightened. She dropped the bottle back into her backpack and was about to start the engine when the snapping of a twig froze her in place.

Bo's words about cougars and bears flashed through her mind. But what made the hairs at her nape prickle was the ever-present knowledge that Karas wanted her dead. She planned to be ready if he made a move.

Spinning, she jammed her hand into the backpack, grabbed the Beretta and brought it up.

The resonant click of a hammer being pulled back froze her in place. "Hold it right there, Missy."

Chapter Three

Pulling back the slide, Rachael brought the weapon up and around. The sight of the man on the horse took her aback. He looked like something out of a western, replete with worn leather chaps, a beat-up western hat, a blue bandanna around his neck—and a rifle the size of a cannon aimed at her heart.

Sitting on the ATV, outgunned in every sense of the word, she held the Beretta steady. Body shot. Centered just to the right of his heart. But she didn't put her finger on the trigger. At the moment, she didn't know if this man was friend or foe. The one thing she did know was that he hadn't been sent by Karas. Judging by the spots on the horse's rump, he was one of Bo Ruskin's cowboys.

"Who are you?" she asked.

Taking his time, he set a gloved hand on the saddle's horn. "I was just about to ask you the same question."

Going with her instincts, she lowered the Beretta. "I'm a guest at Dripping Springs Ranch."

"Since when does Bo Ruskin arm his guests?"

"Since yesterday. And for your information he didn't arm me. I came this way."

The rifle went down. The man threw his head back and laughed. "Well, Bo Ruskin does have some interesting guests, don't he?"

"I wouldn't know," Rachael muttered. Now that the initial burst of adrenaline had ebbed, annoyance that this man had gotten the drop on her set in.

You're getting rusty, Armitage....

"I'm Jimmy Hargrove. Bo's foreman. But I run cattle mostly."

"Rachael Armitage." She unchambered the round and slid the Beretta back into her pack.

"You're pretty good with that, huh?" he asked, referring to the pistol.

"I don't miss, if that's what you mean."

He nodded as if in approval. "Where you headed?"

"Just doing some exploring."

He motioned toward a high ridge to the north. "There's some interesting scenery up that way, especially if you want to put that peashooter you're packing to good use."

"What do you mean?"

He smiled. "There's an area up the valley a ways. Got some old cans you can set up. Makes for some nice shooting."

The thought of some target practice appealed to Rachael. First, because she enjoyed shooting. Second, because she didn't want to get rusty. "I might just check it out."

"Enjoy your stay." Jimmy Hargrove tipped his hat. "Ma'am."

Rachael felt as if she'd stepped back in time a hundred and fifty years as she watched the cowboy ride down the trail and disappear into the scrub. The contrasts between her life in Washington, D.C., and this ranch were enough to give a girl whiplash. She wondered how Bo Ruskin managed out here.

Starting the ATV, she took the vehicle in the direction of the shooting range.

THE STORM CLOUDS began piling up on the western horizon at just before six o'clock. Bo had been working horses most of the afternoon. He'd been bitten once, kicked at and taken a spill. Having gotten little sleep the night before, he was bone-tired. The last thing he wanted to hear when he walked into the house was that Rachael hadn't shown up from her exploration excursion yet.

"That city slicker leave over two hours ago," Pauline explained as she shoved two pies into the oven. "Should have been back by now."

Remembering the way Rachael had torn out of the driveway in that ATV, he shook his head. "She's a little too independent for her own good."

"A lot if you ask me," Pauline put in.

Bo downed a glass of tap water and frowned. The logical side of his brain knew that as a MIDNIGHT agent Rachael Armitage was more than capable of taking care of herself. But well-trained agent or not, she was out of her element on the high plains. She wasn't familiar with the ranch. But what really concerned him was the fact that one of the world's most brutal crime lords had put a price on her head.

"Maybe you ought to saddle up and take a look." Pauline glanced out the window where storm clouds roiled on the horizon. "Looks like it's going to get bad."

"I reckon I'd better." Grabbing his hat, Bo started for the door.

He saddled his most reliable mount—a ten-year-old roan gelding named George— grabbed a slicker from the hook in the tack room and hit the trail at an easy lope.

The ATV's tire tracks were easy enough to follow. The ground was powder-dry. But he could smell the storm. He could feel the electric energy of it in the air. On the horizon a jagged spear of lightning slashed from sky to ground. The ensuing crash of thunder shook the earth. The storm was getting closer. If it rained, the trail would be washed away.

"Damn tourist," he muttered.

Two miles from the ranch, traveling at a good clip over a rocky trail, he heard the unmistakable sound of a gunshot. "Whoa." He stopped the horse and listened. The wind had kicked up, blowing dust and hissing through the treetops. Had he heard a gunshot? Or was it thunder?

A second shot rang out. To the north if he wasn't mistaken. Who was shooting and what the hell were they shooting at? Bo didn't allow hunting on his ranch. He liked the wildlife, wanted to keep it the way it was. But he knew hunters occasionally trespassed onto his land from the adjoining ranch, most of the time without even realizing it. Usually a friendly word or two did the trick.

Only this time Rachael Armitage was out here somewhere. A woman with a contract on her head. Sean Cutter had said she would be safe here. But Bo knew all too well that Viktor Karas had a very long reach.

Another shot rang out, followed by another. Not a sniper rifle, he deduced. A handgun.

As if sensing danger, the Appaloosa danced beneath him. Reaching down, Bo patted his neck. "Easy, boy."

Every sense on red alert, he dismounted and scanned the immediate area. Two more shots exploded. Two hundred yards away.

For the first time in two years, Bo wished he were armed.

But the mere thought caused cold sweat to break out on the back of his neck. The shame that followed was surprisingly keen. At one time, he'd been an expert marksman. He'd won every sharpshooter award a man could win. But Bo hadn't touched a gun since the night Michael Armitage died.

Tying the gelding to the branch of a pinion pine, he crept down a rocky incline toward the source of the shooting. Several more shots rang out. He peeked around a boulder and for the first time had an unobstructed view of the valley floor.

Thwack! Thwack! Thwack!

Shock vibrated through him when he spotted Rachael. She'd assumed a shooter's stance. Legs slightly apart. Right arm straight. Left hand cupping her gun hand. Several tin cans were lined up on a flat-topped rock. One by one she picked them off like target ducks at a county fair.

Worry transformed into anger. Bo had been concerned about her. Evidently, she didn't care. She hadn't bothered to tell anyone where she was going or how long she would be gone. Considering she had a contract on her head, that was downright irresponsible.

But deep inside Bo knew the real source of the hot surge of anger burning through him had more to do with his inability to do what he'd once been so very good at.

Because he didn't want to think about that, he clung to the raging torrent of anger as if it were a life raft. He let it drive him toward her.

Ten yards from her, he growled, "What the hell do you think you're doing?"

She glanced over her shoulder, giving him only half of her attention. "Oh...I was just...killing some cans."

His temper reached the boiling point. "Do you realize there are people back at the house who are worried about you?"

She blinked. "I'm sorry. I must have lost track of time."

"You have a contract on your head, damn it. There's a dangerous storm blowing in." He motioned dumbly at the ATV. "You could have had an accident. Did it even cross your mind that you should let someone know?"

She looked over at the horizon. "It doesn't look that bad."

"Doesn't look that bad out here turns dry creeks into raging rapids and can wash out bridges."

"Look, I'm sorry. I didn't realize it was so late."

He glanced at the Beretta in her hand and the sweat on his back went cold. *Coward,* a little voice chanted. Big bad sharpshooter afraid to look at a teeny little handgun....

"Why are you so angry?" she asked.

"I'm angry because there are rules," he snapped.

She choked back a sound of exasperation. "What rules?"

"This is rugged and isolated country, Rachael. When you go off somewhere, you tell someone. You tell them where you're going and when you'll be back and you stick to the plan."

"I told both you and Pauline where I was going."

"You didn't show up when you told us you would!"

"I said I lost track of time."

He jabbed her shoulder with his finger,

eliciting a flash of anger in her eyes. "Out here, losing track of time can get you killed."

She rolled her eyes. "Now you and Cutter both are overreacting."

Bo could feel his teeth grinding. His heart pounding against his ribs. Unreasonable anger pushing him in a direction he did not want to take. "If that's what you think, you're a bigger fool than either of us imagined."

Her mouth tightened. Stepping toward him, she jabbed a finger into the center of his chest hard enough to send him back a step. "Let's get one thing straight right now, Ruskin. I don't answer to you. This ranch is the last place I want to be. The only reason I'm here is because Sean Cutter forced me."

He brushed her finger away. "Yeah, well, here's a newsflash for you, slick. I'm not going to let you get yourself killed on my watch. You got that?"

RACHAEL STARED into his icy-blue eyes. Anger surged with every beat of her heart. But in addition to being royally ticked off by his attitude, she was also baffled. Bo

Ruskin didn't seem like the kind of man to overreact. In fact, if she weren't mistaken, his hands were shaking. Was he that worried about her safety? Had she given him a bigger scare than she'd initially thought? Or was there something else going on she didn't know about?

The skies chose that moment to open up. The deluge of cold water was so sudden and forceful that it took her breath away. Wearing only a sweatshirt and jeans, she was soaked instantly.

"Come on!" Bo shouted to be heard above the hard rush of rain.

"I've got the ATV," she shouted back.

"Won't make it through Nickel Creek."

"But it'll be ruined, won't it?"

"It'll be fine until the morning." He motioned toward the ridge. "My horse is there. Let's get out of here before that creek floods."

Surprise rippled through her when he took her hand. His hand was large and encompassed hers completely. Rachael got the impression of calluses and strength, but those elements were buffered by warmth and a gentle touch she hadn't expected.

Rain and wind pelted them as they dashed up the incline. At the top she caught a glimpse of a spotted horse tied to a bushy pine. Jake strode to the horse, then turned to her. "Get on and slide back."

"You're going to walk?"

Rain dripped from the rim of his hat. "We're both going to ride. Now get on before we get stranded."

Rachael stepped up to the horse and put her foot in the stirrup. The next thing she knew strong arms shoved her up and onto the saddle.

"Slide back."

Blinking rain from her eyes, she did as she was told. In a single, graceful movement, Bo swung onto the horse and into the saddle in front of her. "Hang on to me," he shouted.

Rachael set her hands lightly on his sides. She got the impression of hard male flesh. Before her brain could process that, the horse bolted into a gallop. She rocked back. Off balance, she grabbed for Bo and put her arms securely around his waist.

The horse took them into a ravine. When Rachael had crossed it an hour ago, the creek had been dry. Now, a foot of muddy water crashed over river rock and sandstone, carrying branches and small debris on a wild ride through the ravine. The horse splashed through the current without a problem.

At the top of the ravine, Bo put the horse into a gallop. Rachael had never felt a horse move like that before. She could feel the animal's muscles flexing beneath her, and the awesome athletic power rendered her awestruck. Even though they moved at a blinding speed, not once did she feel as if she were in danger of falling.

In front of her Bo rode as if he were an extension of the horse. His body was like steel against hers. Rachael could feel his abdominal muscles tense and flex as he moved with the animal.

"Why are we going so fast?" she shouted to be heard above the wind and rain.

"See those greenish thunderheads to the north? We got hail coming."

From the northeastern U.S., Rachael had never seen hail as a dangerous weather phenomenon. The worst she'd ever seen was marble-sized balls of ice. "What's the big deal about hail?"

Bo's laugh carried over the roar of wind. "We get softball-sized hail regularly this time of year. You get hit in the head and you won't be getting up. I lost a couple head of livestock that way last year."

Rachael honestly couldn't imagine the damage such large hail would inflict. But a glance to the north proved the storm was gathering strength. Green-black clouds billowed on the horizon like smoke from some massive fire.

The thought of getting clobbered by a softball-sized piece of ice did not appeal in the least to Rachael. For the first time she realized she had underestimated the power of Mother Nature. It wouldn't happen again.

Rain slashed down like liquid knives as they rode toward the ranch. The sky lowered. Lightning flickered just to the north. The crash of thunder that followed was deafening. The horse continued to move at a breakneck speed.

The storm seemed to chase them. A huge monster, spitting fire and ice. Oddly, Rachael was not afraid. She held on to Bo, her trust in him complete. She knew instinctively he was a competent man. A capable horseman. The kind of man who would get them home safely.

It took twenty minutes for them to reach the ranch. Bo slowed the horse to a jog at the arched gate. Through the driving rain, Rachael saw Pauline and the ranch hand standing at the barn door. For the first time she realized just how worried these people had been, and she felt like a fool.

Bo stopped the gelding at the barn door. "Slide off," he said.

Rachael did as she was told. Bo dismounted and handed the reins to the ranch hand. "Be sure to cool him down slowly. I ran him pretty hard."

"Will do, Mr. Ruskin."

Rachael watched the ranch hand take the reins and begin walking the soaked and sweaty horse up and down the aisle. She had wanted to pet the animal to thank him for getting them to the ranch safely. When she turned back, Bo and Pauline were looking at her expectantly.

"I'm sorry I worried you," Rachael said.

"Were you lost?" Pauline asked.

"No, I—"

"She lost track of time," Bo said sarcastically.

"I didn't think the storm was going to get so bad," Rachael defended.

"Not thinking can get you killed out here," Bo said.

Pauline looked at him sharply. Rachael sensed she, too, was wondering about the source of his anger. Had he been sincerely worried about her? Or was there something else in the works?

Tipping his hat, Bo turned and started for the house.

Pauline's gaze met Rachael's. Within the brown depths of her eyes, Rachael thought she saw the woman apologizing for her surly boss. Before she could say anything, Pauline turned away.

Rachael stood in the aisle and watched both of them walk away.

"WHERE ARE YOU?" Standing at the window in his study, Viktor Karas looked down at the people scurrying about Moscow's Teatralnaya Square with a keen sense of disdain and waited for an answer.

"Minneapolis."

"Have you located the target?"

Ivan Petrov's voice wafted from the speakerphone on the conference table. "She's in the state of Wyoming, not far from the city of Cody. I'm on my way there now."

Karas's eyebrows went together. It wasn't often the American government surprised him. But this came as a total shock. He'd expected the MIDNIGHT Agency to hustle Rachael Armitage into protective custody at one of their safe houses. That would have been much more convenient. Four months ago, he'd paid nearly two million dollars for the list of locations the federal government used to protect their most precious witnesses. Finding his son's murderer was worth the cost, but he hated that the money had been spent in vain.

"How do you know this?" Karas asked.

"I…interrogated one of the mechanics who works at the hangar where the Cessna took off."

"But even the most lowly employees of the MIDNIGHT Agency have high security clearances. How did you get him to talk?"

"I threatened to murder his wife and children, of course."

A surge of anger had Karas gripping the

phone more tightly. "You idiot. He will go straight to the authorities and our plan will be foiled."

"The mechanic I spoke to will never talk again, Mr. Karas. I cut out his tongue and then I killed him."

Viktor Karas closed his eyes as relief settled over him. It wasn't often that he was impressed with an employee, but he was with this young man. "A man will do anything to protect his wife and children."

"Including selling his soul."

"Wyoming is a large state," he said, his mind already jumping ahead.

"My recourses are extensive," Ivan Petrov returned.

Karas smiled, pleased that he'd chosen this young man for the job of finding his son's murderer. "How close are you to finding her?"

"I know she's with a former MIDNIGHT agent by the name of Bo Ruskin. I'll know where she's staying by the end of the day."

Despite the alcohol, Viktor Karas's heart began to pound. "Tell me about this Bo Ruskin."

"He's a former MIDNIGHT agent. Sniper.

Some undercover work. Left the agency two years ago. That's where I lost track of him."

"Why did he leave the agency?"

"He was involved in a shooting. Details are scarce, but whatever happened prompted him to resign."

Karas sipped vodka from his crystal tumbler, his interest in Bo Ruskin piqued. "Americans are a weak lot."

"Except for when it came to Nikolai."

Karas closed his eyes at the mention of his beloved son. "My boy will not rest in peace until she is dead, Ivan."

"I understand."

"Find her. Do it quickly."

"The only thing that has slowed me down, Mr. Karas, are the flights."

"Have you slept?"

"I do not need sleep."

Karas smiled. "Call me the instant you know where she is."

"Of course, Mr. Karas."

Viktor Karas hit the speakerphone button. Staring out the window of his office, he sipped his vodka and thought about all the ways he could kill Rachael Armitage.

Chapter Four

Bo sat on the porch swing and tried hard not to think of Rachael. He tried directing his thoughts to more productive topics. The branding that needed to be done tomorrow. The training tactics he would use on the difficult young stud he'd been working with in the round pen. All the work that needed to be done around the ranch.

But time and time again, his thoughts drifted back to her. The way she'd looked at him as he'd berated her for being irresponsible earlier in the day. Big green eyes laced with caution and a hefty dose of attitude. Hair so tawny and glossy his fingers itched to touch it. A mouth so sexy he could barely think straight every time he looked at her.

He recalled the way her body had felt pressed against his on the wild ride to the ranch. She'd been all warm, wet curves and so soft it had taken every bit of control he possessed not to turn in the saddle and pull her to him.

He started when the screen door slammed. Bo looked up to see Rachael approach. When she spotted him, she hesitated, then ventured toward him with the caution of a skittish horse. Her expression told him the conversation they were about to have was a duty she needed to get out of the way.

"I owe you an apology," she said. "For being late."

"It was a long day," he said. "I shouldn't have dressed you down like that."

"It was irresponsible of me to lose track of time the way I did. I didn't think."

"Apology accepted."

She arched an eyebrow. "That's it? No lecture? No yelling?"

"Got that out of my system earlier." Trying not to notice her scent, he looked away. "It's up to you to decide if you're going to heed my good advice."

"That was way too easy, Ruskin. You're getting soft in your retirement years."

He glanced her way. She was wearing a dark turtleneck and faded jeans. Even though it was cold, her feet were bare. He stared at them a moment, noticing her toenails were painted cherry-red. Damn, even her feet were sexy.

He'd accepted her apology without comment so she would leave him alone.

Evidently, she wasn't finished. "May I sit?"

"Sure." He scooted over a little too quickly, a little too far.

She settled onto the swing beside him. Pulling her knees up to her chest, she wrapped her arms around her legs. "It's chilly."

"Nights are cool up here this time of year." But his mind wasn't on the temperature, and he wasn't the slightest bit cool. In fact, he'd broken a sweat beneath his denim jacket. All he could think was that she smelled of sandalwood and sweet musk. He breathed in deeply, savoring what he should not.

"You probably know this already, but I'm

not very good at following other people's rules," she began.

"I gathered that."

"I'm used to doing what I want, when I want, and I'm not very subtle about it," she continued. "In case you haven't noticed, I'm a bit of a hard driver."

"I've noticed." An owl hooted, and he looked into the darkness. "Cutter thinks you have a death wish."

"He's wrong. He just—"

"Tolerates your kamikaze tactics because you're a good agent," Bo finished.

"I get things done," she said somewhat defensively.

Bo couldn't help it. He laughed. "Yeah, well, your ability to get the job done aside, Cutter cares about you. If he didn't, you wouldn't be here."

She dropped her gaze to her hands. "In any case, I just wanted you to know I didn't mean to appear irresponsible today. I'm really not an irresponsible person. I just tend to be…independent."

Independent was an understatement, but Bo didn't say as much. He didn't want to get into the reasons for her penchant for recklessness. He didn't like the way he was reacting to her. He didn't want to have to talk to her any longer than necessary. Not because sitting out here on the porch with her was unpleasant, but because she was making him feel things he didn't want to feel—and tempting him to do things he knew he would regret.

Mike Armitage had been his best friend. Being attracted to his widow felt wrong. Especially when Bo had been the one to pull the trigger....

"It's a whole different world out here than in the city," she said after a moment.

He risked a look at her, and immediately wished he hadn't. Her eyes glittered like the moon on a restless lake. Even in the dim light, he saw wariness in her expression. The soft curve of her mouth. A fragile jaw. His blood surged low and hot when he noticed moisture on her lips. For the umpteenth time he wondered what it would be like to kiss her. He wondered if her kiss would be sweet or spicy or somewhere in between. He wondered if she would pull away or lean into him for more....

Bo rose abruptly. "It's late. I've got an early day tomorrow."

She rose just as suddenly, as if his abrupt movement had startled her. "Oh. Sure." She wiped her palms on her jeans. "Bo, I'm used to being busy and I'm not afraid of hard work. If there's anything I can do around here…"

Stop looking so damn sexy.

"Get with Pauline," he growled and walked into the house without looking back.

RACHAEL LEFT the house just as the sun broke over the eastern horizon, streaking the sky with slashes of crimson and gold. Donning running shoes and a sweatsuit, she pounded down the trail at a speed that was far too fast for this early in her morning-ritual run. But her mind was troubled. Over the years she'd found that physical punishment was the best cure.

An hour earlier she'd wakened to total darkness, her heart hammering, her body slicked with sweat. It wasn't the first time bad dreams had interrupted her sleep; over the years her profession had elicited nightmares. But the dreams that had jolted her that morning had nothing to do with her job, and everything to do with a cowboy with cool blue eyes, a slow drawl and the kind of mouth that could make a girl question her self-imposed vow of going it alone.

For two years her hormones had been dormant, frozen like a delicate sapling during a long, hard winter. Since her arrival at the ranch, however, it seemed the spring thaw had set in and her hormones had arisen with a vengeance. It was a complication Rachael could do without.

She needed to stay focused and keep her mind on her goal of bringing down Viktor Karas, even if, because of Cutter, that goal had been put on hold. The last thing she needed was to get sidetracked by Bo Ruskin. After all, she was only going to be at the ranch for a few days, a couple of weeks max.

"You are *not* attracted to Bo Ruskin," she panted.

She'd sworn after Michael's death that she would never get involved again. At least until Viktor Karas was behind bars— or six feet under. Rachael might be a risk-taker, but she would never put her heart on the line again.

She drove herself hard down the trail. Around her, the pinion pine and juniper stirred restlessly. Finches and sparrows chattered in the treetops of the taller ponderosa pines. Rachael maintained a punishing pace. Her quadriceps burned as she muscled her way up a steep incline.

At the top, lungs on fire, she stopped to catch her breath. Bending at the waist, she put her hands on her knees and gulped air. As her heart rate and breathing slowed, she began to notice the stunning beauty of her surroundings.

To the north a vast yellow plain dotted with scrub stretched as far as the eye could see. Beyond, the purple ridge of Bareback Mountain sat like some sleeping sentinel. To the east, the ridge dropped to a valley dissected by a meandering stream. It was there that she spotted the two men on horseback moving a small herd of cattle.

She recognized Bo's spotted horse immediately. But more than the spots on the animal's rump, she recognized the man. The tall way he sat in the saddle. The graceful way he moved with the horse. As if he himself were part of the animal.

Rachael reached for the binoculars in her backpack and put them to her eyes. Sure enough, Bo and one of the ranch hands were taking a small herd of cattle through the creek toward the grassy plain to the north.

She told herself she'd grabbed the binoculars merely to identify the riders. But her eyes lingered on the man in the black hat. Bo Ruskin rode a horse as if he'd been born in the saddle. He was masculine grace and balance rolled into a single, hard-bodied package that was all too easy on the female eye.

"You're an idiot, Armitage," she muttered.

Annoyed with herself for letting her imagination run amok, Rachael lowered the binoculars and shoved them back into her backpack.

Refusing to give the two men a second glance, she turned away from the valley and pushed herself into a run.

IVAN PETROV had always enjoyed killing. Ever since that thrilling first time when he was fourteen and had to defend himself in that Moscow back alley. It wasn't until he was eighteen that he realized he could get paid for it.

He was immensely pleased with himself as he strode down the main street of Cody,

Wyoming, and browsed the shops. Most were western wear. Native American jewelry. Saddlery and tack for the many ranchers who came into town to buy wares. Cody was a nice, all-American town. One where a Russian man with an accent and ponytail would stand out. So an hour ago Ivan had ducked into a quaint barbershop and had his hair cut military-short. In the western wear store next door, he'd bought jeans, boots and a hat. The getup looked dudish, but so did half of the other people walking the street. He was good at blending in when he wanted to.

It was almost noon when he entered the small bed-and-breakfast at the edge of town. He'd registered under the name John Miller. But his stay would be a short one. By tomorrow at this time, Rachael Armitage would be dead and he would be on his way to Moscow to collect his pay.

In his room, Ivan used his cell phone to dial Viktor Karas's number. "I am in Cody, Wyoming," he said without preamble.

"Do you know where she's staying?"

Ivan Petrov smiled. "Bo Ruskin owns a ranch north of here."

"Nothing came up when I did a property search."

"It's not in his name."

"So how did you find him?"

"Bo Ruskin entered a rodeo competition last year." Ivan had been inordinately pleased when he'd stumbled upon the information while surfing the Internet. "Bull riding. Ruskin won a belt buckle for riding a bull called Bone Cruncher."

"Such a benign error in judgment." Karas sounded pleased. "He hasn't been with the agency for two years. Are you certain she's staying with him? It's not above Cutter to throw up a couple of red herrings."

Remembering the cowboy he'd shared several drinks with at the local bar, Ivan smiled. "Ruskin owns the Dripping Springs Ranch. She's there, Mr. Karas. I'm happy to take care of both problems for you, sir."

Silence hissed over the line for several heartbeats. Long enough to make Ivan's nerves tingle. Then Karas said, "I want the woman alive. Ruskin, too."

Disappointment grated, but Ivan endured it. He'd been looking forward to killing the woman. The man, too, if he got in the way. But he knew that to disappoint

Karas now would be a mistake. Especially over something so petty. Sooner or later, he would get his chance.

"But the American government is watching you, sir."

Karas smiled. "Let them watch."

Ivan didn't understand. "What do you want me to do?"

After a lengthy pause, Viktor Karas answered.

And Ivan the Terrible smiled.

Chapter Five

Bo wiped the dust from his face and watched the cattle cross the dry creek bed and head toward the north pasture, where the grass hadn't been grazed since fall. He whistled at the cow hand helping him, and motioned toward the house, telling him his work was done for the day. It had taken them exactly five hours to move seventy head of cattle and it was barely noon.

Bo had just turned his mount toward the house four miles to the west when the cell phone clipped to his belt vibrated. Even before answering it, he knew who it was. Grimacing, he answered with a curt utterance of his last name.

"One of my aircraft mechanics was found this morning with his tongue cut out," Sean Cutter said without preamble. "He refueled your Cessna when you were here. Chances are, he knew where you were heading."

The significance of the words hit Bo like a punch. "Karas?"

"We don't know. But this mechanic died a slow and painful death. If he'd glanced at the flight plan you filed, he talked."

"Tortured?"

Cutter sighed. "I've seen a lot, Bo, but this is the worst thing I've ever seen in my life."

Dropping his head, Bo rubbed his temples. "What else?"

"His wallet was taken. Credit cards. Cash. ID."

"Could it have been a robbery?"

"It's possible," Cutter said. "Or maybe someone wants it to look that way. You and I have been around long enough not to take any chances."

Bo silently agreed. "I flew directly to the airstrip here at the ranch."

"I know," Cutter said.

The silence that followed said it all: Viktor Karas could very well know Rachael Armitage's whereabouts.

"You have someone watching Karas, though, don't you?" Bo asked.

"Like a hawk. He was sighted in Moscow just this morning."

"He has a lot of thugs working for him. Maybe he sent someone."

"Maybe."

"You don't sound too sure."

"You know as well as I do that isn't his style."

Bo did know, and even though he was sweating beneath his denim jacket, a chill swept through him. When a situation became personal to Viktor Karas, he handled the killing himself. He would dole out whatever revenge he saw fit personally. And he would enjoy every ugly moment of it.

"He's hands-on all the way," Bo said bitterly.

"We're going to have to operate under the assumption Karas knows about the ranch."

Bo's curse burned through the line. "What about Karas's Learjet? Is it still in Moscow?"

"The Lear left the airport in Moscow two days ago."

"Flight plan?"

"Athens, Greece."

Bo figured they both knew the jet had not landed in Athens. "You have men on the ground there?"

"Yeah. They're working with Interpol. But there's no sign of the jet."

"You're certain Karas is in Moscow?"

"We used a high-powered scope, spotted him inside his apartment on Teatralnaya Square."

Bo felt marginally better knowing Karas was several thousand miles away. But something about the situation didn't feel right. "So what do we do in the interim?"

"I'm going to send a chopper to pick up you and Rachael."

"Damn it, Cutter."

"I'm sorry, Bo, but I'd rather have you unhappy than dead. This is the way it's got to be."

"ETA?"

"Give me two hours."

Bo disconnected and looked out over the vast land he'd come to love in the last two years. Before Cutter's phone call, the place had been peaceful. Now, he saw menace in the vastness, danger in the high forests and open plains.

And deep inside he suddenly knew that keeping Rachael safe was going to be a hell of a lot more dangerous than he'd ever anticipated.

THE HOUSE WAS oddly silent when Bo walked in. Usually, Pauline was in the kitchen, cooking or cleaning, with the radio blaring. But this afternoon, the kitchen was dark. Pauline was nowhere in sight. Concern clamped down on him like a vise when he realized he hadn't seen Jimmy, either, who was usually working in the pens or mucking stalls this time of day. Where the hell was everyone?

"Pauline," he called out. "Rachael?"

Worry augmented into a cold, gripping uneasiness when neither woman answered.

The Lear left the airport in Moscow two days ago.

Cutter's words scrolled through his mind. The thought that followed sent a cold claw of fear scraping up his spine.

Cursing beneath his breath, Bo burst into the living room. "Pauline! Rachael!"

But no one was there.

Bo never panicked; the emotion was simply not part of his persona. But he could feel it burgeoning inside him now. He crossed the room at a run and took the stairs two at a time to the top. He was so intent on finding the women safe and sound, he didn't see the shadowy figure emerge from the bathroom and plowed into it at full speed.

A distinctly feminine grunt sounded. The figure reeled backward. Bo reached out just in time to break her fall, but his legs tangled with hers. He stumbled, lost his balance—and came down on top of her.

He got the impression of soft curves and wet skin. Damp fabric against his dusty clothes. An exotic fragrance that reminded him of some tropical fruit wafted up from bare flesh.

"What the hell do you think you're doing?"

It registered that he'd found at least one of the women he'd been concerned about, but for an interminable second all he could think about was the feel of her beneath him. Soft. Warm. Curvy. Wet. The kind of woman a man wanted to sink into and not come up for air for a week.

"Ruskin, you are so dead." Rachael's voice reached him as if from a great distance. "Get off me before I hurt you."

It took his befuddled mind several seconds to come up with an appropriate response that didn't include kissing or caressing. When he finally spoke, his voice was angry and thick, his words far from brilliant. "I called out for you, damn it. Where the hell were you?"

"In the bathroom," she snapped. "That's where people go when they take a shower."

She smelled good enough to eat in a single bite. Bo's mouth began to water. Raising up on his elbows, he looked down at her. Her hair was damp and spread out behind her like wet silk. Moisture glistened on bare flesh. She was wrapped in one of his towels....

Oh, boy.

Realizing he'd gone hard, he scrambled off of her and offered his hand. "I didn't mean to knock you down."

"Wouldn't have happened if I'd been dressed." But she looked flustered as she rose. "What has you in such a big hurry, anyway?"

Bo knew better than to indulge in the moment. But his eyes took on a life of their own and flicked down the front of her. He'd seen plenty of half-dressed women in his time. But he'd never seen one that looked half as good as Rachael Armitage did in that towel. Her arms were long and well-muscled. He could see the cleavage of generous breasts where she'd tucked the corner of the towel. The towel itself came to midthigh, revealing long runner's legs. Suddenly, the urge to peel away the towel and get a look at the woman beneath was every bit as powerful as his need for his next breath.

Bo's mouth went dry. Forcing his gaze back to hers, he noticed her cheeks were tinged pink. That she looked uncomfortable. He was acting like an idiot. And she'd noticed.

"Get dressed," he growled. "We're leaving."

"What?" Her eyes narrowed on his. "What are you talking about? What happened?"

"I just got a call from Sean Cutter."

Her eyes widened, but it wasn't fear he saw in their depths. It was interest. Anticipation. An odd kind of thrill elicited by danger. He knew because he'd experienced all of those things himself back when he'd been an agent. At the moment, it scared him.

"Where's Pauline?" he asked.

"She went into town to buy apples for pies."

"You seen Jimmy?"

"He drove her. He needed a few things."

Bo stepped back, refusing to let his eyes drop again. He wasn't sure what he would do if he gave himself the chance to screw this up. "Get dressed and come downstairs."

Without waiting for a response, he turned and walked away.

RACHAEL WAS SHAKING when she walked into the guest bedroom and pulled the door closed. She tried telling herself it was anger that had her heart pounding, her hands fluttering like hummingbird wings. But that didn't explain why her entire body still tingled with pleasure from Bo Ruskin's touch. It might have been over two years since she'd been aroused, but she recognized the signs. That she was vulnerable to her own hormones scared her more than any armed criminal.

Throwing on jeans, a sweatshirt and boots, she left the bedroom and went downstairs. She found Bo sitting at the kitchen table, staring into the cup of steaming coffee in front of him.

He looked up when she entered. "I made coffee," he said.

Because she wasn't quite ready to make eye contact, Rachael went to the counter and poured. "What's going on?" she asked.

"The mechanic who refueled my Cessna in D.C. was murdered," Bo said.

Rachael stopped pouring, her mind spinning through all the terrible implications of that. "How?"

"He was tortured to death."

"For information?" She asked the question, but she already knew.

Bo nodded. "Cutter called to warn me there's a possibility Karas knows you're here. He's sending a chopper to pick us up."

The words shook her. Not because she was afraid. Rachael had been waiting for a shot at Karas for a long time. It was the not knowing that disturbed her; she didn't like not knowing where he was or what he was up to. If he came for her, she wanted to be ready.

She met Bo's gaze levelly. "Instead of running, maybe we ought to use this opportunity to get the son of a bitch."

"Not on my watch."

"Bo, it's me he wants. You know I'm the perfect bait. This could be the opportunity we've been waiting for."

"My mission is to keep you safe."

"This isn't about you or your mission. It's about me and Karas and a little thing called justice."

"I'm not going to get into a war with Viktor Karas."

"Too late," she said crisply. "He's already declared war. On me. On the MIDNIGHT Agency. On anyone who gets in his way. I've been fighting this war for two years and this is the best shot I've had at him since it started. I don't plan to run away."

Bo scrubbed a hand over his jaw. Rachael heard the scrape of his whiskers and found herself remembering the way those same whiskers had chafed her face when he'd been on top of her....

"Cutter was specific," Bo said. "My objective is to keep you safe and alive. We will not engage Karas or his men."

Rachael set down the coffee without drinking it. "With all due respect, Ruskin, I don't take orders from you."

"With all due respect to you, when I'm responsible for your life, you do." He rose and approached her. "You're getting on that chopper one way or another."

Rachael could feel the anger building inside her, like a thunderhead filled with rain and about to burst. "Cutter is getting soft. He's overprotective. Overreacting. Overlooking a major opportunity. Bo, he's going to blow the best chance we've had."

"Cutter knows what he's doing, Rachael. You have to trust in the system—"

"The system is what got Michael killed!" she shot back.

He stiffened, blinked at her.

She hadn't meant to say it. Until that very moment she hadn't even realized she felt that way. Only then did she accept the possibility that for two years now she'd been dealing with something much more unwieldy than simple grief.

The screen door slammed.

Bo spun. Rachael reached for her sidearm—only to realize she hadn't brought it downstairs with her.

Pauline walked into the kitchen with two bags of groceries in her arms, her eyes level on them. "I'm not even going to ask if I'm interrupting," she said, setting the bags on the counter.

Bo shoved his hands into his pockets. "Pack an overnight bag," he said. "You're leaving."

"What?" Pauline's eyes widened and flicked from Bo to Rachael and then back to Bo. *"¿Qué pasa?"* What's happening?

"All I can tell you is that if you stay here at the ranch, you're in danger," he said.

"Because of her?" Pauline shot a glare at Rachael. "I knew she was trouble the moment I laid eyes on—"

"Because of my former job," he interrupted.

Turning, Pauline angrily started putting the groceries away. Bo walked to her and put his hand on her shoulder. "There's no time for that," he said quietly.

When Pauline turned toward him her eyes were sober. "Are you in danger?"

"We're all in danger if we stay." He squeezed her shoulder gently. "Pack an overnight bag. I'll have Jimmy drive you in to Cody so you can check into a hotel. I'll cover all the expenses—"

"It's not the expense I'm worried about *Señor* Ruskin." Her gaze lingered on Rachael long enough for Rachael to see the dislike in them. "It's her."

The last thing Bo wanted to do was put his employees in danger—or referee a cat fight between two women he cared for and admired. He already had one death on his conscience; the thought of anyone else getting hurt made him queasy.

"You're going to have to trust my judgment on this, Pauline."

The woman didn't look happy about it, but she nodded.

Bo only hoped he was able to get everyone out of there before all hell broke loose.

WITHIN THE HOUR the ranch was vacated. Jimmy took the Tahoe and drove Pauline into town. Bo turned out the horses, so they could forage on grass for a few days. The chopper should arrive any minute now.

If he could only figure out what to do with Rachael Armitage…

He couldn't stop thinking of the way she'd felt beneath him when he'd been on top of her in the upstairs hall. It had been a long time since he'd been that close to a woman, and she'd made one hell of an impression. Soft flesh. Intriguing curves. A scent he couldn't get out of his head.

The reality that she was Mike's widow taunted him. The truth of what happened that night haunted him with renewed fervor. It was the ultimate irony that this woman—a woman whose husband had been gunned down by his own hand—had entered his life again…and he was attracted to her beyond anything he'd ever known.

He didn't have to ponder how she would feel about the ugly role he'd played in her husband's death. He knew. Just as he knew she would hate him for it even if he did have the truth on his side.

"I can't believe we're running."

He nearly jolted at the sound of her voice. Turning, he found her standing in the center aisle of the barn with her backpack in her hand. "We're not running," Bo growled. "We're doing the smart thing and playing it safe."

"Playing it safe isn't all it's cracked up to be. Just ask Michael."

He felt himself flush, the old pain cutting him with the proficiency of a blade. "You're not the only one who lost him."

"He was my husband."

"He was my best friend." *And I'm the one who fired the killing shot.* The words dangled on the tip of his tongue, but Bo didn't speak them. He wouldn't, either. But there was a small part of him that believed she deserved to know the truth. Sooner or later she would find out. What would she think of him then?

"I didn't mean to bring up Michael." She sighed. "I'm sorry."

"You have nothing to be sorry for." The words came out more harshly than he'd intended.

"It's just that…I've been thinking about him a lot lately."

"Me, too." Because he couldn't speak of Mike and want his widow at the same time, he looked around the deserted barn, hating it that he couldn't meet her gaze.

The distant *whop! whop! whop!* of a

chopper's rotor blades broke the silence. Rachael's eyes met his. Within their depths he saw anger. Frustration. Most of all, he saw disappointment. In the agency. In Sean Cutter. In him. There was nothing he could do about any of those things. The only thing he could do was keep her alive and pray she didn't hate him when all was said and done.

"Let's go," he said.

Without speaking, she turned and walked out of the barn. Bo followed. Standing in the gravel driveway, he looked toward the horizon. Sure enough, the dark shape of a Bell 207 chopper came into view.

"Where's he going to put it down?" Rachael asked.

"There's room right here in the driveway."

The chopper made a pass. Grinning, Bo raised his arms and gave the signal for a landing, letting the pilot know he could put it down right there.

The chopper circled around and returned. Dust kicked up as the craft lowered. Forty feet. Thirty...

The blast struck him like a flaming,

speeding truck. One moment he was waiting for the chopper to touch down, the next he was flying backward into space. Bo landed on his back, hard enough to knock the breath from him. Debris pelted him as he sat up, hot missiles traveling at a high rate of speed. Something slammed into his shoulder hard enough to send him back down.

But Bo barely felt the pain. All he could think of was the woman whose life lay squarely in his hands—and the people who'd perished on that chopper.

Chapter Six

A groan ripped from Bo's throat as he scrambled to his feet. He looked around, his heart hammering like a piston. The area looked like a war zone. The twisted fuselage lay on its side twenty yards away, smoke billowing. A piece of the rotor lay on the ground next to it.

"Rachael!" he shouted.

Seconds earlier, she'd been standing behind him. *"Rachael!"* He heard fear in his voice now. Felt that same fear zinging through his body. *"Rachael!"*

"I'm...here."

He spun to find her sitting on the ground a few yards away. Several emotions struck him at once. Relief that she was alive. Concern because she was bleeding. A powerful need to protect. But all of those things were tempered by a cold terror that crept over him like a wave of ice water.

He rushed toward her. "How badly are you hurt?"

But her own injuries seemed to be the last thing on her mind. Her eyes were on the smoking remnants of the fuselage. "The pilot." Her voice shook. "Bo...we need to see if there were any survivors."

He glanced down at her leg. A piece of sheet metal had struck her, cutting through the fabric of her blue jeans and into her flesh. She was bleeding, but not with life-threatening profusion.

"Is your leg broken?" he heard himself say.

She shook her head. "I'm just...cut."

"Stay put. I'm going to check for survivors. Don't move until I look at that wound. You got that?"

Bo started toward the downed aircraft. For the first time it struck him that the catastrophe could have been sabotage. This kind of destruction was Viktor Karas's style. Violent. Spectacular. Carefully orchestrated for powerful effect. But how could the crime lord have managed it? Had one of his thugs planted a bomb in the aircraft before it left the hangar? Or did he have someone on the ground here at the ranch who took the chopper out with a ground-to-air missile?

The thought made the hairs at his nape prickle. He looked around uneasily as he approached the craft, but saw no sign of life through the rising tendrils of smoke. He tried the hatch, but it was jammed. Taking a deep breath, he kicked it open and looked inside.

Bo had seen death before. Too many times if he wanted to be honest about it. But the ugliness of it never ceased to shock him. Both the pilot and copilot were deceased.

Closing his eyes briefly, he choked back a wave of nausea. He quickly checked the radio, but it was badly damaged by fire. "Damn," he muttered as he backed from the craft.

He should have known better than to think Rachael would heed his request that she stay put. He found her standing near the barn, her cell pressed to her ear.

Without hesitation, Bo crossed to her, took the phone from her hand and snapped it closed.

"What are you doing?" she asked angrily.

"Keeping you from getting sloppy."

Her eyes flicked to the devastation of the crash, and he saw her blink back tears. "The agency needs to be notified," she said. "Those men...their families..."

"We use the phone inside," he said. "Karas probably already has it bugged. But we don't want to clue him in on the location of the cell towers here."

But they both knew Karas already knew everything he needed to know in order to kill them both. It was only a matter of time.

She jerked her head once, but didn't take her eyes off the smoldering fuselage. The urge to comfort her was strong, but there wasn't time. Taking her shoulders, he turned her toward the barn. "Get in the barn." *Just in case the house is next,* he thought darkly. "I'll make the call."

He could feel her trembling beneath his hands. The sight of the crash had obviously shaken her badly. Him, too, if he wanted to be honest about it. But if they wanted to live, there was no time to mourn those who had died.

"We can't let that son of a bitch get away with this," she said.

"We won't." Giving her shoulders a final squeeze, Bo sprinted to the house. Inside, he grabbed the kitchen phone and hit the speed dial for Cutter's secure line. The other man picked up on the first ring.

"Where's my chopper?" Cutter asked without preamble. "It disappeared off radar two minutes ago."

"The chopper is down," Bo said.

Cutter's curse burned through the line. "What about my men?"

"There were no survivors."

The silence that followed stung Bo's ears, and he knew the other man was thinking about the agent and pilot he'd lost. About the families he would be notifying. And in that moment Bo didn't envy him his job.

"What the hell happened?" Cutter asked.

"The chopper exploded just as it was about to touch down. There was no warning."

"Mechanical failure?"

"Cutter, there's too much damage to tell, but I'm betting there was either some type of explosive device on board or else Karas hit it with a rocket launcher or ground-to-air missile."

Cutter made a low sound in his throat. Bo felt the other man's fury coming through the line. "If there was a bomb on board, you can bet there was GPS."

"Probably," Bo agreed.

"We have to assume Karas knows where you are. That he knows Rachael Armitage is there. Get the hell out of there, Bo. Now."

"We're leaving now."

Bo heard muffled conversation between Cutter and someone else, then Cutter came back on the line. "We received a call less than two minutes ago from someone claiming to be part of Karas's organization claiming responsibility for the crash."

Now it was Bo's turn to curse. Brave and decent men had died today. Impotent rage coursed through him at the senselessness of their deaths. "Can you pick him up?"

"We need proof. We're watching him. He's still in Moscow. We're working with Interpol to try and get it done, but the Russian authorities aren't known for being cooperative."

The thought of international red tape working in Karas's favor infuriated him.

"Don't worry," Cutter said. "We'll get him."

Bo thought of Rachael and the lengths the kingpin would go to in order to get his hands on her. "Do you have a contingency plan for Armitage?"

"We'll come get her. But we'll have to inspect all of our aircraft first. That's going to take some time." He paused. "You got somewhere to go? Somewhere out of sight?"

"Yeah, but you know as well as I do he'll find us sooner or later."

"Okay. Get the hell out of there. Stay out of sight from the air. We'll find you via the GPS transmitter in your cell."

"Roger that."

An instant before Bo disconnected, Cutter surprised him by saying. "Be careful, man."

"I don't do things any other way."

BO FOUND RACHAEL sitting in a plastic chair in the barn. She rose when he entered, but it wasn't the female warrior that approached him. She looked shocked. Scared at best. He glanced at the wound on her thigh and grimaced. The blood had soaked through the fabric and now reached all the way to her knee.

"I'm going to need to take a look at that," he said.

Squaring her shoulders, she looked down at the blood and shrugged as if the wound on her leg was nothing more than a scratch. "Tell me what Cutter said."

Bo strode briskly into the tack room and snagged the first-aid kit off the shelf. "He told us to get the hell out of here."

"Karas?" she asked.

He didn't want to answer; he knew if she found out Karas had just murdered two MIDNIGHT pilots, she would claim one more reason to go after him. But there was a part of him that knew he owed her the truth.

"Someone claiming to be part of Karas's organization called and claimed responsibility while I was on the phone with Cutter," he said.

"That bastard." Striding away from him, she slammed the heel of her hand against the wall. "Did they pick him up? For God's sake, they know where he is."

"They're working on it."

"That's bull."

"This has got to be by the book."

"The Russian authorities are protecting him."

Bo didn't reply. Instead, he stood there for a moment, watching her pull herself together. "We've got to go, Rachael. Now."

She turned angry bright eyes on him. "Are you crazy? We can't run. We can't let him get away with this."

"We don't have the resources here at the ranch to do much of anything."

"Why can't Cutter send another chopper?"

"He's going to do just that. But every aircraft has to be inspected for bomb material first. You know protocol."

"What are we going to do?" she snapped. "Put our tails between our legs and run?"

Bo motioned toward the two horses in the corral. "I'm going to saddle those two horses and we're going to ride to an old homestead a few miles to the north and wait this thing out."

"You're kidding."

"I'm sure you have a better idea," he said dryly.

"How about if we stay here and blow the hell out of Karas the moment he sets foot on the property?"

Bo couldn't help it; he smiled. But the moment of humor was short-lived. There had been a time long ago when he would have reacted much the same way. Back when he'd been a younger man and hungry to prove himself as an agent, he would have been champing at the bit for a go at a crime lord like Viktor Karas.

Experience had taught him caution.

He studied the woman standing across from him, annoyance warring with admiration. She was ready to take on the world all by herself if she had to. She might be a good agent—fast on her feet and brave as hell—but she was no match for Viktor Karas.

How are you going to keep her safe when you can't even bring yourself to pick up your weapon?

The question was a brutal reminder of his limitations. He hadn't picked up a rifle since the day he'd shot and killed his best friend. Truth be told, he wasn't sure he could.

"I'm going to pack a few things." He walked to the tack room and tossed her a bag. "I suggest you do the same."

Rachael held her ground in the barn. "You're wrong about this, Bo."

"Not the first time," he said and started for the door.

SWEAT BROKE OUT on Bo's neck as he pulled the long leather sheath from his bedroom closet. He laid it on the bed and unzipped the case. The Remington model 710 stared up at him like a steel snake full of venom and about to strike. Gritting his teeth, he pulled the rifle from its sleeve.

For two years the weapon had sat untouched. He hadn't been able to clean it or even look at it without getting cold chills. Viktor Karas was going to change everything.

Damn Sean Cutter for putting him in this situation....

A chill passed through Bo the instant his fingers came in contact with the synthetic stock. Setting the rifle on the bed, he ran his finger down the barrel and he couldn't help but think that the last round that had passed through it had ended the life of a man who'd once been his best friend. The husband of a woman who had no idea what had gone down that night.

Knowing better than to let his mind take him there, Bo went back to the closet and tugged out the ammo box. He sat it on the bed, opened it and removed an extra box of shells and two grenades. Tucking both into one of the saddlebags, he picked up the rifle, slid it into its sleeve and yanked the zipper tight. He slung it over his shoulder, picked up the saddlebag filled with supplies and headed back to the barn.

He found Rachael standing in the aisle with the other saddlebag at her feet. She looked up when he approached and not for the first time he was taken aback by her beauty. Bo tried hard not to remember how good she'd felt beneath him just over an hour earlier. He tried even harder not to imagine how she would react once she found out the truth.

"All packed?" he asked.

She lifted the dual saddlebags he'd given her. "Weapon. Ammo. Bottled water. Some food. And the first-aid kit."

Setting his saddlebag on the ground, he snagged two halters from the tack room and took them into the pen for two horses. He cross-tied the animals in the aisle, then proceeded to saddle them. Once they were saddled, he lashed the saddlebags to the saddle skirt, then buckled the rifle sheath in place.

"What now?" Rachael asked.

"We ride." He crossed to the left side of the horse. "Come here."

She approached him with the caution of a young fox approaching a trap.

"Put your left foot in the stirrup. Your right hand on the horn. And swing your leg over his rump."

She was an athletic woman and mounted without a problem. But athletic or not, he could see she was not an equestrian and made a mental note not to go too fast—unless he didn't have a choice.

"We're going to ride at a fast clip," he said.

She looked at him skeptically. "I'm not a very good rider."

"Hang on to the horn with your right hand. Keep him on a loose rein. This gelding is a solid mount and knows what to do. He'll take care of you."

Bo mounted. "I'll take a look at your leg once we get where we're going."

She nodded. "And where's that?"

"There's an old homestead a few miles from here. We'll ride along a dry creek bed where the trees will give us cover."

"You think Karas or his men are in the area? With a chopper or what?"

"Could be."

He nudged his horse forward, and they left the barn and entered a small corral. Bo carefully maneuvered the horse alongside the gate and opened it without having to dismount.

"You're good at that," Rachael said.

"You train horses the right way and they give it all back to you when you ride." He glanced out at the land beyond, listening. "Keep your eyes open for aircraft."

"All right."

"Ready?"

She gripped the horn and gave a nod. "Now I know how you must have felt when you rode that bull."

"Let's go." He nudged the horse into an easy lope.

He could hear Rachael's horse behind him. He'd chosen the most reliable and steady mounts he had. He only hoped that made up for her lack of riding skills. The ride to the dry creek bed was over open country; they would be sitting ducks. He had a terrible feeling the ride wasn't going to be leisurely.

He led the way at a fast clip. His horse moved like a finely oiled machine beneath him, his gait as smooth as a rocking chair. He glanced at Rachael. Her concentration was wholly on the horse beneath her. She wasn't a bad rider, but he could tell she was struggling to maintain her balance and keep a solid seat.

There was nothing he could do. One of the most violent and powerful kingpins in the world wanted her dead. Bo wasn't in any shape to protect her. All they could do was run....

"You okay?" he yelled at her.

She gave him a dark look. "How much farther?"

"Three miles, give or take."

"Lovely."

The words were barely out of her mouth when the low rumble of an engine rose above the roar of wind in his ears. Bo glanced over his shoulder. Disbelief slammed into him when he saw a chopper hovering over the house. Disbelief transformed into horror when the house erupted into a massive orange fireball that billowed thirty feet into the air. Debris flew in all directions. Thick, black smoke darkened the sky.

"They're behind us!"

Rachael's shout came to him as if from a great distance. He couldn't take his eyes off the destruction of the place he'd called home for the last two years. It had been his sanctuary. His refuge. Now it was gone.

"Bo!"

Her scream yanked him from his reverie. Only then did it register that the chopper was swinging around as if to come toward them. Shock transformed into cold stark terror. The horses were running all-out now, but they were no match for a chopper. With the line of cottonwood trees still two hundred yards away, he and Rachael were as good as dead.

He veered toward Rachael. For the first time he saw fear in her eyes. He felt that same fear jumping through him with every wild pound of his heart.

"Hang on!" he shouted. "Give him some rein! Let him run!"

Knowing her horse would follow his, he pushed his gelding faster. He could hear the chopper behind him now. The ground blurred by. Wind roared in his ears. He glanced at Rachael, saw her leaning low against the horse, hanging on for dear life. If she fell now it would be bad. He prayed that didn't happen.

Rifle fire punctuated the thought.

Two years ago, Bo would have unsheathed his rifle and taken a few potshots at them, just for good measure. Now, the thought froze him with fear. That he couldn't make himself do it shamed him. Made him realize he was not capable of keeping this woman safe. He should have told Cutter he was suffering with hoplophobia. Fear of firearms. Had been since the day he shot and killed his best friend....

The chopper blew past. Dirt kicked up around both horses as the sniper on board tried to take them out.

"Son of a bitch!" Bo yelled, furious at the thought of them shooting one of the horses.

They were twenty yards from the trees when the chopper swung around for a second pass. Bo scanned the tree line. He searched his memory for a place they could hide. In the rainy season, flash floods cut a deep grove in the sandy soil, forming temporary caves. Some were twenty or so feet deep. Enough to give them temporary cover from a sniper's bullet.

But if the chopper landed they would be pinned. Once they ran out of ammo, Karas's men would be on them like wolves on lambs....

The chopper bore down like a giant bird of prey. Dust billowed all around. Bo urged his horse faster and glanced up. The aircraft was so close he could see the muzzle of the sniper's rifle sticking out of the hatch.

He risked a look at Rachael. She was riding low, hanging on for her life. A volley of gunfire erupted. Bo saw her horse shudder. Rachael's scream tore through the air when the animal stumbled. Bo caught a glimpse of blood on the gelding's shoulder. He watched helplessly as horse and rider went down.

"Rachael!"

The horse went to its knees with such force that its nose plowed into the earth. Rachael went over its head and landed hard on her stomach. Bo swung his mount around and streaked toward them. A few feet away from her he vaulted from the horse. But he knew the chopper would be back to finish the job.

He looked toward the horizon. Sure enough the chopper was bearing down on them at a stunning rate of speed. Digging into the saddlebag, Bo removed one of the grenades. The hairs on the back of his neck stood on end when he faced the chopper. He could practically feel the crosshairs burning into his chest. The urge to toss the grenade was strong, but still he waited. In his peripheral vision he saw Rachael crawling toward him. Relief slid through him when the fallen horse got up and shook himself.

Still, Bo didn't move. He gauged the speed of the chopper and the distance between them. Mentally he counted the seconds. He wondered if the pilot would make another pass and try to shoot them down or if they would land the craft and try to take Rachael to Karas. The thought sickened him.

In the next instant it was clear the pilot was going to stop and hover over them. Dust and small debris kicked up as the chopper got closer. The horses grew restless. Bo tightened his grip on the grenade.

"Toss your weapons and no one gets hurt!" a voice called out from a loud-speaker.

Bo didn't hesitate. Turning back to his horse, he unsheathed the rifle and tossed it to the ground five feet away.

"Put your hands up and walk away from the woman."

He knew once he put some distance between him and Rachael, the sniper on board would take him out. They wanted her alive and wouldn't dare risk shooting her or face the wrath of Viktor Karas. In that instant Bo decided he would die before he let them take her.

Concealing the grenade in his palm, Bo put up his hands and backed away from her. The chopper shifted and he knew the pilot was listening to the sniper on board and lining up for a shot. He'd done the very same thing himself too many times to count in the years he'd worked for the MIDNIGHT Agency.

"Come closer, you son of a bitch," Bo whispered.

The chopper hovered twenty feet off the ground, about fifty feet away. Slowly, the pilot maneuvered the aircraft closer. Forty feet. Thirty. At twenty feet, the aircraft began to slowly rotate. The hatch came into view. It was open; Bo saw the black steel of the sniper's rifle. *I used to be you,* he thought, and took his one and only chance.

Chapter Seven

Bo pulled the safety pin and threw the grenade with everything he had. The sniper spotted the grenade as it sailed into the hatch. He yelled something to the pilot, but it was too late. The sniper dropped his rifle and scrambled for the grenade. The chopper began to regain altitude.

The explosion sent the craft into a wild spin. It tilted at a precarious angle. One of the rotors struck the ground, kicking up debris and dust. Pieces of shrapnel and steel flew at them like hot, flaming missiles. Ever aware of Rachael just a few feet away, possibly injured, Bo rushed toward her.

To his surprise, he found her in a shooter's stance, gripping her pistol in both hands, her eyes on the faltering aircraft. She never got the opportunity to shoot.

"Get down!" he yelled.

She looked at him just as he reached her. "What—"

Bo took her down in a protective tackle, turning just in time to ensure she landed on top of him. Pieces of smoldering steel and plastic landed all around as he rolled to cover her body with his.

As suddenly as the situation had exploded out of control, everything went stone still. Bo was aware of her beneath him. Trembling violently, but undeniably alive. Twenty feet away, the horses snorted and jigged, but showed no sign of running away. The chopper had been reduced to a smoldering heap of twisted steel.

"You can get off me now."

He looked down at her, inordinately relieved that she was unhurt. She was lying on her back. Propped on his elbows, he was squarely on top of her. Gazing into her eyes, something powerful and protective stirred deep inside him. Something else that was wholly male shifted low in his gut.

"Are you all right?" he asked when he found his voice.

"I haven't decided yet."

He rose on legs that weren't quite steady and extended his hand to her. "You took a hell of a fall."

She accepted his hand. "It wasn't enough to keep me from reaching for my weapon."

The subtle accusation stung. But Bo didn't let himself react. The truth of the matter was he deserved it. The situation had called for him to engage. To remove the rifle from its sheath and open fire at the attacking chopper the moment it was within range. He hadn't done that. Hadn't been able to react even though both their lives had been in mortal danger.

Because he didn't know how to respond without opening up a can of worms he had no desire to deal with—because the truth was too damn shameful to admit—he turned away and walked toward the horses.

Evidently, she wasn't ready to let it go. "You didn't follow protocol." Following him, she tapped on his shoulder. "You let them get too damn close. You—"

His temper reached its flashpoint. He

swung around to face her. "I stopped them!" he said, gesturing toward the wreckage.

She blinked as if his sudden outburst of anger surprised her.

Bo pulled himself back. But he was thinking that he should have tried harder to evade this assignment when Sean Cutter had asked him to do it. He should have told Cutter the truth. That he was afraid to pick up his gun. Hadn't been able to do so since he'd shot and killed this woman's husband. His best friend. Now, she was in danger and he didn't know how to protect her.

That was when he noticed the scratch on her cheekbone. He let his gaze drop and skimmed the rest of her. Her jeans were torn at the right knee. He could see blood soaking into the fabric from where she'd been cut by shrapnel back at the house.

"You're hurt," he said.

"I've got a few scratches."

He glanced at the horses. His eyes went directly to the blood on her gelding's shoulder. Concern swept through him as he crossed to the animal.

"Easy, boy," he said as he picked up the reins.

The Appaloosa spooked, but relaxed the instant Bo got close. Speaking softly, he examined the injury. It looked as if a bullet had grazed the animal, leaving a deep cut in the skin.

"Oh, no," Rachael said, coming up beside him. "He's been shot."

"It's a graze, but deep." Blood dripped down the animal's shoulder onto the dry earth. "He's going to need a few stitches."

"Can you do that?"

"Not here." He looked into her eyes. "You know as well as I do Karas's men will be back. I'll lay odds there's GPS onboard that aircraft. He isn't going to let this stop him. His men are expendable."

She looked uneasily around, her hand going to the butt of the pistol in her shoulder holster. "We're sitting ducks here."

"We need to get to the homestead." Bo glanced at the wreckage where black smoke rose into the air. "I need to check for survivors first. If we're lucky, Karas will be onboard."

He figured they both knew the kingpin wasn't. Karas didn't place himself in dangerous situations. He had a whole army of men for that. All Karas did was run the show. A deadly show to be sure.

Bo didn't think he would find any survivors. The crash had been too violent. The aircraft itself was barely recognizable. He didn't want to see what waited for him inside, but he didn't have a choice.

"I'll be right back." Handing the horses' reins to Rachael, he started toward the downed craft.

The fuselage had shattered on impact. The Plexiglas windows had been blown out. The rest of the craft had burned. A small fire crackled beneath a piece of sheet metal. He could smell Jet A fuel.

But there were darker smells, too. Steeling himself against the carnage, Bo took a deep breath and pulled back a large piece of sheet metal. He closed his eyes at the sight of the pilot's body. The sniper's body lay a few feet away. It had been ejected upon impact. He hadn't survived.

Bo took a few minutes and looked through the wreckage for anything they could use, but he found nothing.

"Anything?"

He faced her. She was staring at some point beyond him, her face pale, her expression grim. The body of the sniper, he realized.

"Don't look at it," he said.

She blinked as if waking from a nightmare. "I've seen death before."

"Yeah, but it never gets any easier. Come on."

When she didn't move, Bo took her arm and guided her back toward the horses. "Let's get out of here."

"My God, Bo, that man—"

"Don't think about it." He didn't let her go until she was standing beside the wounded gelding. "Get on."

"We need to call Cutter."

"Not out in the open like this."

Her eyes went to the wound on the gelding's shoulder. "But he's hurt. Can he be ridden?"

Bo nodded. "It's not a life-threatening wound. I'll take care of him once we get where we're going."

EVEN THOUGH THE MEN who'd died in the crash had tried to kill her and Bo, the sight of their broken and burned bodies shook Rachael to her core. It wasn't the first time she'd seen death; she'd had more than one close encounter with the grim reaper since she'd been with the MIDNIGHT Agency. But to see death up close and personal made her realize just how fragile and precious life was.

To make matters worse, the wound on her leg was beginning to hurt. The bruises and lacerations she'd sustained in the fall from the horse were coming to life with a vengeance. At some point her head had begun to pound.

For the last twenty minutes they'd been riding within the tree line of a dry creek bed. Bo kept the horses at an extended trot. Rachael had noticed right away that her gelding was limping. The horse didn't seem to mind too much. It was as if the animal knew his job and was determined to do it despite his injury. But she felt badly for the animal.

"Are you hurting?"

She looked over to see Bo ride up next to her. Concern laced his expression.

"I'm okay." She reached down to pat the gelding's shoulder. "I'm more worried about him."

Bo glanced at the horse. Rachael saw affection in his eyes and knew he would never let anything happen to the animal. "Horses are amazingly tough animals." One side of his mouth curved. "Besides, he knows I'll get him patched up once we stop."

His gaze went back to her and his eyes narrowed. "You're favoring your shoulder."

Realizing she was, Rachael straightened, but it was no use trying to hide the pain. She'd landed hard on the shoulder when the horse fell. Her EMT training told her she hadn't dislocated it, but in the last hour the joint had grown stiff. She was pretty sure there was a nasty abrasion beneath her jacket.

"I landed on it when the horse fell," she said.

"You hurt anywhere else?"

Rachael shook her head, but she ached all over. She didn't even want to think about what she looked like. Not that she cared, she quickly reminded herself. But several times she'd caught herself brushing dirt from her clothes, wiping blood from the minor cut on her cheek. Silly thing to be thinking about when she'd come within an inch of getting shot down like some prized doe.

"How far to the old homestead?" she asked.

He pointed toward a high ridge dead ahead. "Just beyond that ridge, there's a valley. A creek runs through the valley. It's mostly dry this time of year. There's an old house and barn just on the other side."

"Hidden?"

"There are trees. Plus it was built into the side of a hill."

"The house is underground?"

"Partially."

"So Karas and his thugs won't be able to detect our presence using infrared."

He nodded. "It's nothing fancy, but it should keep us out of the line of fire for a few hours."

"Hopefully until Cutter can get a second rescue chopper out here."

Rachael tried not to think about how long that might take. She tried even harder not to think of all the terrible things that could happen in the interim.

THE LIKENESS was unnerving. Viktor Karas could have been looking into a mirror, into his own eyes, his own face.

But he wasn't.

The makeup artist had taken a little over an hour and cost him close to five thousand American dollars. But it was well worth the time. Viktor Karas now had a body double.

"All right, Mr. Karas, your turn."

They'd met at a small office building on the south side of Moscow in Sasha Ogalov's studio. Sasha, the makeup artist, was the best in all of Russia and worked the theaters of Moscow and St. Petersburg. Viktor Karas never settled for anything but the best.

His body double, Andrei Lokov, was a small-time hoodlum who'd worked for him going on two years. Karas had made the mission clear: fool the American agents who were watching him into thinking Andrei was him so he could travel to the United States.

He took the chair Sasha offered. "I want to look like a fat American," he said.

She laughed, a practiced sound that grated on his nerves. "We'll have to put some extra padding on you, Mr. Karas. You're anything but fat."

He smiled, but she annoyed him. He'd told her if she did a good job, he would reward her by taking her to the United

States with him. To Hollywood where she could work her makeup artistry on the big-screen celebrities. All she had to do was turn him into someone else.

What Sasha Ogalov did not understand was that Viktor Karas never left loose ends.

"I want red hair," he said. "A big belly. And a cowboy hat."

Sasha laughed again. "John Wayne with red hair. I can do that."

He studied the wall of photos as she draped the sheet over his shoulders and went to work coloring his hair. Once the color was set, she presented him with contact lenses and, finally, the clothes he'd had custom-fitted and tailored just a week before.

The transformation took just over an hour. When Viktor Karas stood and looked into the full-length mirror, he found himself looking at a fat American stranger. A man who would blend in with American society. A man the CIA would not follow when he walked out of this office building.

"You do excellent work," he said to Sasha.

"Thank you."

"My flight is scheduled to leave in an hour."

Her face brightened. "I'm already packed."

"Excellent." He smiled at her. "Why don't you grab your bag and I'll call a taxi?"

She brought her hands together. "Thank you, Mr. Karas."

Sasha started toward the back room of the small studio. With slow deliberation, Viktor Karas withdrew the tiny chrome pistol from his waistband. With expert precision he pulled back the slide and fired two silenced bullets into her back.

She made a sound that sounded like a kitten's mewl. Then she fell with the grace of a fallen figure skater.

Karas turned to his body double.

The man stared back at him. Wide blue eyes filled with fear. Karas smiled to put him at ease and handed the man his cell phone. "I want you to walk out of the building and get into my car. Tell my driver to take you to my home. Call my office on the way and tell my secretary to call a meeting for eight a.m. tomorrow morning."

"Yes, Mr. Karas."

Viktor Karas reached out and touched the man's shoulder. "The American CIA must believe you are me. Give them no indication otherwise. Understood?"

The man jerked his head so hard his jowls quivered. "Yes, sir."

Viktor Karas pulled a cigar from his jacket pocket and lit the tip. "Excellent."

His body double left.

Glancing at the Rolex strapped to his wrist, Karas blew a perfect smoke ring into the air.

THE OLD HOMESTEAD loomed into view like something out of a western movie. Constructed of rough-cut wood and composite shingles, the house was built into the side of a hill. The front porch sagged like a swaybacked nag. The front door hung at a cockeyed angle, held up by a single hinge. Three multipaned windows dotted the front of the house, but there was no glass to be seen in a single pane.

Rachael had been hoping for a vacant house with running water and electricity. The house went beyond old, and the only thing running inside it was probably mice.

"I'll bet you bring all the girls here," she said.

Despite the situation, Bo grinned. "Just the ones I want to impress."

He stopped his horse in a small dirt area between the house and the only standing outbuilding. The yard had once been encircled with a picket fence, but the wood had long since rotted, leaving a trail of broken pieces.

Rachael took it all in with a sense of relief that they would only be there a couple of hours. Turning in the saddle, she scanned the tree line that surrounded the homestead. Because of the huge canopies of the cottonwoods that grew along the creek, the front of the house would not be visible from the air.

Bo dismounted and stretched. She did the same and followed him to the open door of a ramshackle shed row. The small building had three sides and a roof. But there were holes the size of a man's finger in the roof, broken boards that let in more sunlight than they kept out. The entire building sloped precariously.

But someone, a very long time ago, had deemed this place beautiful enough to build here. Rachael had never been unduly interested in old houses or antiques or even history for that matter. But the thought of some young couple starting their lives together here intrigued her.

"How old is this place, anyway?" she asked.

"Just over a hundred years old."

"I wonder who the original owners were." She wasn't really expecting an answer, so it surprised her when he replied.

"Lucas and Amelia Ruskin built this place back in 1904."

Ruskin.

She smiled at him. "Your great-grandparents?"

He looked at her over the horse's saddle, but his eyes were shadowed by the brim of his hat. "Great-great-grandparents."

The thought of a family holding on to a piece of land—a piece of their heritage—for more than a century gave her a warm feeling in the pit of her stomach. "How long did they live here?"

"Until they died. There used to be a dirt road that came out this way, but over the years people stopped using it and the land reclaimed it."

"So your family has owned this place for more than a hundred years."

"Not exactly."

She cocked her head, intrigued.

"My great-great-grandparents lived here until they died in 1934. My mother had moved to Great Falls and auctioned off the ranch and livestock." He lifted a shoulder, let it fall.

Rachael thought about that a moment. "So you bought this place back after sixty years?"

"Two years ago, it came up on the auction block. I needed a place to live." He shrugged again.

The same year her husband had been killed. The same year Bo resigned from the MIDNIGHT Agency. "So you bought the ranch and moved into the house after the shooting."

He looked away. "Yeah."

She thought of the explosion and felt a quiver of sympathy for him. He'd lost more than a house. He'd lost part of his heritage. "I'm sorry about what happened to your house."

He gave her a wry smile. "I have good insurance."

"There are a lot of things insurance can't replace."

At that moment she wanted to see his face; she wanted to know what he was thinking, what he was feeling. But he lowered his head slightly and the brim of his hat cast his face into shadow.

He led the horse into the dilapidated barn. Removing the bridle, he used the halter and lead to tie the animal to a sturdy beam and proceeded to untack him.

Rachael led her horse to the beam and did the same. As she worked to unfasten the saddle, her eyes were drawn again and again to the wound on the horse's shoulder. She stroked the animal. "It's going to be okay, boy. Bo is going to fix that right up for you."

"I think he likes you."

She turned to find Bo standing right behind her. He was standing so close she could smell the leather from his jacket. The out-of-doors scent of his clothing. At five feet six inches, she was not a small woman, but he seemed to tower over her and she guessed his height to be at least six feet four.

Inexplicably, she blushed. "How can you tell?"

She jolted when he set his hands on her shoulders and nudged her closer to the horse. His hands felt incredibly strong and steady. The horse lowered his head and rubbed his face gently against her.

"He doesn't do that to just anyone," Bo said.

She looked into his eyes. "He's selective about who he gives his affections to."

His gaze never wavered. "Very."

Suddenly all she could think of was the moment back at the house when they'd collided. The seconds when they'd been lying on the floor and his face had been mere inches from hers. In that moment something powerful had occurred between them. Something Rachael didn't want to acknowledge but could not deny.

Shaken by the feelings rising in her chest, she turned quickly away. She knew he was wondering about her reaction. Maybe even about his own reaction to her. But she couldn't explain. Not even to herself. Bo was the first man since Michael who'd made her feel anything. He made her feel alive. Made her feel like a woman.

But the reawakening was not welcome. Not now. Life was simpler without the complication, and Rachael had no desire to deal with it.

"I'm going to check out the house." Without waiting for a reply, she turned and fled.

Bo wasn't sure exactly what had transpired between them a moment ago, but he didn't stop her. He tried not to think about her as he treated the wound on the gelding's shoulder. But his mind refused to cooperate. As much as he didn't want to acknowledge it, he was attracted to Rachael Armitage. He was attracted to her the way he'd never been attracted to another woman.

How would she react if she knew he was responsible for her husband's death?

"She's going to hate you, buddy," he growled.

Both horses raised their heads and looked at him. Bo smiled. "Who asked you guys anyway?"

He spent the next ten minutes tossing grain and pumping water from the old well. When the horses were bedded down—and he ran out of things to do—he headed for the house.

He found Rachael standing at the kitchen window, staring out at the vast country beyond. She turned and looked at him when he entered.

"How's the gelding?" she asked.

"He's going to be fine."

There was a tension in the air that hadn't been there before. A tension Bo didn't want to acknowledge. He sure as hell didn't want to acknowledge its source.

"I wonder how many times your great-great-grandmother stood at this window and looked out across the land?"

The question surprised him. He didn't see Rachael as the kind of woman who got sentimental about stuff like that. Then again she kept surprising him. And he knew she was a woman with a lot of layers, all of them protected by a tough outer shell. "A lot, I imagine," he said.

"What made you decide to buy the ranch back?"

I couldn't handle my job after I shot and killed Mike.

The words hovered on the tip of his

tongue, as deadly as any bullet. But looking into her eyes, he couldn't say the words. He knew that made him a coward. But as much as he didn't want to admit it, he wasn't sure he could handle this woman hating him.

"I needed something to do when I left the agency." Dropping his gaze, he shrugged. "The ranch was for sale."

She contemplated him as if trying to see all the things he held inside. Within the depths of her eyes, he saw questions. Questions he had no desire to answer.

Before she could ask them, he motioned toward the bloodstain on her thigh. "I need to take a look at that wound."

She glanced down as if she'd forgotten about it and stared at the bloodstain. He thought she would argue, but she didn't.

"You're going to have to take off your pants," he added.

"I was trying to think of a way around that."

He went to the saddlebag and removed a small camping blanket and handed it to her. "Wrap yourself in this. I'll get the stove set up and heat some water. We packed the first-aid kit."

Taking the blanket, she disappeared down

the narrow hall. Bo busied himself unpacking the small camping stove. It wouldn't
cast much light or warmth, but it would have
to suffice since they couldn't build a fire. He
was in the process of opening the first-aid
kit when Rachael appeared in the doorway.
She had the blanket wrapped around her
hips.

Bo's eyes ran the length of her. Even
dusty and disheveled she was one of the
most beautiful women he'd ever laid eyes
on. Like he needed to be thinking of that
at this moment.

"Have a seat," he said, patting the
rickety kitchen table.

Gripping the blanket with a white
knuckled hand, Rachael complied. "I tried
to get a look at the wound, but there was a
lot of dried blood."

"I'll get it cleaned up for you." Picking
up a gauze pad, he turned to her. She was
sitting on the table, her eyes level with his.
For an instant he couldn't speak. All he
could do was look into her bottomless
green eyes and hope he didn't fall right
into them.

After a moment, he gave himself a hard
mental shake and looked down in the

general direction of the wound. "Just part the blanket a little bit so I can take a look."

Carefully, she spread the blanket. Bo tried not to notice the silky white thigh that came into view. Then he spotted the wound and his focus came rushing back. It was a clean cut about two inches long with a good bit of bruising and swelling.

"You got hit pretty hard," he said.

She nodded. "Yeah."

"Probably a piece of metal. You could use a few stitches."

"I don't think I want you sticking a needle in me."

Dabbing the wound with an antiseptic gauze, he smiled. "Since I'm fresh out of needles, a butterfly bandage will have to suffice." He raised his gaze to hers. "You'll need a tetanus shot when we get back."

She nodded.

He cleaned the wound as thoroughly as he could. Most of the MIDNIGHT agents were EMTs, but Bo was having a difficult time keeping his focus on the wound. Every time he touched her all he could think of was silky flesh and firm muscles and one of the prettiest legs he'd ever seen.

What little concentration he had evaporated when she spoke. "You haven't talked about what happened that night."

The statement hovered unacknowledged for several interminable moments. Bo's mind spun through all the lies he'd conjured, but he couldn't speak the words. He couldn't lie. But he couldn't tell her the truth, either.

He looked into her eyes, and the words nearly tumbled out. But he held his tongue. All the while her gaze searched his for answers. Answers she would not like. Answers that would make this woman hate him, the way he'd hated himself for the last two years.

"It was a tough scene," he said in a rough voice.

"I've been there," she said gently. "I can handle it."

All he could think was that she couldn't. He sure as hell hadn't handled it very well. He wasn't sure any human being with a conscience could ever handle something like that.

A chirping sound reached him through the fog of his thoughts. After a moment, he realized it was his cell phone. Stepping away from her, he dug into his coat pocket. "You're good to go," he said.

She pulled the blanket over her leg. "Thank you."

Turning away from her, he answered with a growl of his name.

"Ruskin. This is Mike Madrid."

Something in the other man's voice gave him pause. Bo had a sixth sense when it came to knowing when something was wrong. And he knew Mike Madrid was going to hit him with something he wasn't prepared to hear. "What is it?"

"MIDNIGHT Headquarters was just bombed," Madrid said.

Chapter Eight

The meaning of the words registered slowly in a brain that didn't want to believe. Disbelief and a deep sense of violation rose inside Bo. The MIDNIGHT Agency was a top-secret organization. Very few people knew of its existence, even fewer knew where the agency headquarters was located. How the hell could something so catastrophic happen?

"Casualties?" he heard himself ask.

"Going to be heavy."

Bo knew it was bad when cool-headed Mike Madrid sounded shaken. "What about damage?"

"The blast was powerful, took everyone by surprise. Most of the second floor is gone. Dozens of people are missing. A dozen more are hurt badly."

"Cutter?"

"Missing."

Bo cursed. "Missing in the rubble or missing as in someone took him?"

"All we know at this point is that there's no sign of him anywhere."

"He was in the office?"

"He'd logged in." Madrid sighed. "Look, we've got a lot of chaos right now. Phone system is down. Cops and feds and Homeland Security are on the scene. Acting director initiated a Code ninety-nine."

The initiation of a Code ninety-nine indicated an emergency situation, alerting and activating all MIDNIGHT agents. Bo wasn't an agent. But he knew in his gut this involved him. He knew it involved Rachael Armitage. Just as he knew Sean Cutter had probably been the target....

"I'll lay odds that Viktor Karas will take responsibility for the bombing." The words elicited a slow rise of fury.

Madrid was silent. Bo could hear chaos in the background now, sirens and shouting and a male voice barking out orders. "This is his style. Hit hard and fast and unexpectedly. Take what he wants then get the hell out."

"The collateral damage is a bonus."

Bo had turned away from Rachael, but she was circling him, watching him. She knew something was wrong and wanted to know what it was.

"Cutter was supposed to send a chopper out here once the fleet was inspected," he said.

"Not going to happen, Bo. Whoever did this hit the hangar, too. Half the aircraft are gone. The other half will need to be inspected for explosives. We lost at least one pilot. Another is still unaccounted for."

"Karas knows where we are," Bo said.

"Then I suggest you get the hell out of there."

The suggestion made him feel like a coward. Two years ago Bo would have made a stand. He would have told Madrid they'd be waiting for Karas when he showed. It shamed him that his own fears kept him from doing what he knew needed to be done. "I'm going to get off the line, Madrid. I don't want anyone picking up this signal off the cell tower."

"Sure."

"Keep me posted on Cutter, will you?"

"Roger that."

Bo snapped the phone closed.

"What the hell is going on?"

Bo looked at Rachael. Her eyes were wide and questioning. She looked pumped up and ready to pounce on him. He wondered how she would react to learning Cutter was missing. But deep inside he knew. She was going to want to go after Karas.

"MIDNIGHT headquarters was bombed," he said.

She stiffened as if steeling herself against a blow. But he didn't miss the physical ripple that went through her body or the flash of rage in her eyes.

"How could that happen?" she asked. "HQ is one of the most secure places on earth."

"Karas is connected. He's a brutal son of a bitch. He's capable of anything to get what he wants. Including torturing some cleaning or administrative person to get information."

"My God." Setting her fingers against her temples, she rubbed. "Tell me everything you know."

"Cutter is missing."

"Missing or kidnapped?"

He shrugged, knowing at this point they had to consider worst-case scenario.

Spinning away from him, she slapped her palm down on the old table, bringing a rise of dust. "Sick bastard."

"Madrid said he'd call as soon as they find Cutter."

"But you don't think they will."

He said nothing. The silence that followed spoke more loudly than a thousand words.

She closed her eyes briefly. "You know what Karas is capable of."

"Cutter was probably the primary target."

"My God, Bo, they'll torture him."

He didn't respond. The prospect of Sean Cutter at Viktor Karas's mercy was not a pleasant thought. Cutter might be one of the strongest men Bo had ever met, but no one was above Karas's unparalleled brutality.

"We can't let Karas kill Cutter. We can't let him get away with this."

Setting her hand on her pistol, she began to pace. Bo watched her traverse the small kitchen. She'd gone into warrior mode. Her mouth was tight. Her expression set and furious. He could feel the rage building inside her like a storm. It was as if at that moment she didn't even realize he was in the room.

"There's nothing we can do," he said.

She stopped and turned to him, her eyes blazing. "The hell we can't."

"You're his number-one target, Rachael. He wants you to take the bait. I'm not going to let you play right into his hands."

"I'm not going to sit around and let them torture a good man to death. Karas wants me. I say we give him what he wants."

"Now you're talking crazy."

"Don't treat me like I'm some stupid rookie," she snapped.

"Then stop acting like one."

Another layer of fury entered her eyes. "I'm tired of running from him, Bo. Now he has Cutter. We can't let this stand."

"If you get reckless, he's going to win this thing."

"I'm a trained agent, damn it. I know what I'm doing. I'm not going to sit on my duff while this bastard takes out more people I care about."

"Yeah, well, here's a newsflash for you, tough guy. You're not in charge. I am. And I'm not going to let you do something stupid."

She took a step toward him. "What's your brilliant plan?"

"We wait this thing out."

"Why didn't I think of that?" she said sarcastically.

"It's a hell of a lot smarter than all that fire I see in your eyes."

"What you see in my eyes is something you don't see when you look in the mirror."

The barb cut. Bo tried not to react; he'd sworn he wouldn't let her get to him. But his temper unfurled. "If you've got something on your mind maybe you ought to just say it."

"You're scared of Karas. I don't know what got into you back there, but you acted as if your rifle was on fire. You didn't pick it up when you could have—"

"Enough!" he roared.

His voice seemed to rattle what little glass remained in the windows. For several seconds, they stood there, breathing hard, staring at each other like two contenders facing off in a boxing ring.

"I've been shot at," he said. "I've had my house blown up. I was forced to kill two men back there."

"It's part of the job," she pointed out.

"I'm no longer an agent."

Her eyed burned into his. "Once an agent, always an agent."

Realizing they were edging onto a topic that was best left alone, Bo sighed, reined in emotions he never should have let himself feel. "Look," he began in a more reasonable voice, "you have one pistol. Limited ammo. No backup. I have a pistol and a rifle and a single grenade left. We're several hundred miles from the nearest MIDNIGHT agent. We don't know if we can trust local law enforcement. And you want to take on Viktor Karas?"

She got in his face. "So you're suggesting we sit here and wait for Karas and his goons to storm the place in the middle of the night?"

"I'm suggesting we don't confront the most powerful criminal in the world with a couple of peashooters and your badge of honor! That's crazy!"

"Crazy is better than being a coward."

The words struck a direct hit and Bo

felt it all the way to his core. He stared at her, his heart pounding. In some small part of his mind, he wondered how she would react if he told her he was the one who'd shot and killed her husband. If taking the life of his friend was reason enough for him to have walked away from the agency.

"I'm going to bed down the horses for the night."

She said something to him as he headed toward the door, but Bo couldn't make out the words over the hard hammering of his heart. The rush of blood through his veins. He was angry. Furious, in fact.

Worse, he was ashamed because she was right.

RACHAEL HADN'T MEANT to say it. As far as she was concerned, calling someone a coward was one of the worse things you could say. She could tell by the way he'd flinched that she'd struck a nerve. Bo Ruskin might be cautious, but he didn't have a cowardly bone in his body. Not even close. The truth of the matter was, she owed him an apology.

"Damn," she muttered, walking to the window and leaning against it.

It wasn't the first time her temper had gotten the best of her, and she'd said something in the heat of an argument she was sorry for later. Still, she didn't understand his willingness to walk away from Karas.

He'd accused her of being a hothead. That had struck a nerve, too. It was the reason Cutter had put her on mandatory leave and forced her into protective custody. But Rachael recognized the fact that after Michael's death, she *had* become more of a risk-taker. She'd become more spontaneous in the way she operated. She'd schooled herself not to analyze her actions too closely. Had she taken it too far?

Six months after Michael's death, the agency shrink had deemed her ready for work. Deep inside, Rachael had known she wasn't. She'd told the shrink what he'd wanted to hear, but within her a dark need for revenge seethed.

Michael had been working undercover inside Viktor Karas's organization. He and Bo had set up a brilliant sting. But the sting had gone wrong, and Michael had ended up dead. At that point, all of Rachael's priorities had shifted; she'd focused all of her attention on bringing down the son of a bitch who'd murdered her husband and stolen her future. She'd developed tunnel vision on Karas without so much as a thought to her own safety. In the last two years, she'd had some close calls, taken some risks she shouldn't have. Her colleagues began to notice. In the end, Sean Cutter busted her.

And now here she was, holed up in this old homestead in the middle of nowhere with a man who would just as soon let Karas slink back into his hidey-hole with the rest of the vermin. Not Rachael. She wanted Viktor Karas's head on a platter for what he'd done.

It didn't elude her that Bo Ruskin had been there the night Michael died in that bloody shootout. It was the last operation of Ruskin's career. She knew in a way that only a kindred spirit could know that what went down in that warehouse was the reason Bo had walked away.

She stood in the kitchen, pondering that, and watched the dust motes swirl in the fading light coming in through the window. Bo had been in the barn now for twenty minutes. Damn him for being so cautious, so reasonable. She needed to apologize for calling him a coward.

She busied herself unpacking her saddlebag and setting the contents on the kitchen table. She'd just set out her spare weapon when Bo appeared at the door.

Rachael took in the tall length of him. The snug jeans, leather jacket and black hat that shadowed his eyes. She wanted to attribute the flutter in her stomach to the discomfort of her impending apology; it was so much easier than facing up to its real source. But her attraction to Bo Ruskin was the one thing she did not want to acknowledge.

"I'm sorry for the things I said," she began. "I crossed a line. I had no right."

He set his saddlebags on the table. "We're on the same side, Rachael."

"I know. But I want Karas."

"We all want Karas."

"To different degrees."

"You're going to have to accept that we have different methods of achieving our goal and respect my decision on how to handle this situation."

"Bo, I can't stand the thought of Cutter being tortured to death because he's the only person who knows where I am."

"Cutter may not talk."

But they both knew Karas would not stop until he did.

For several minutes she watched him unpack. He'd come prepared. He'd brought a small camping heater. Several military-type boxed meals called MREs or Meals-Ready-to-Eat. A couple of blankets. The first-aid field kit. Water in a collapsible container.

"So what do we do now?" she asked.

He glanced out the window at the growing darkness beyond. "We pack it in for the night. Wait for someone from MIDNIGHT to contact us."

She hadn't wanted to hear that, but there was nothing she could say or do that would change the situation. "I'm sure it will come as a surprise to you if I tell you I've never been good at waiting."

His mouth twitched. "I'm shocked."

She turned away before he could see her smile.

But the moment of humor was short-lived. Rachael's heart slammed against her ribs when the *whop! whop! whop!* of a chopper's rotors cut through the silence.

She spun, her gaze snapping to Bo's. "The agency?" She was already starting toward the door to have a look.

Bo reached out and stopped her by grasping her arm. "It's not the agency," he said.

"How do you know?"

"MIDNIGHT uses Bell Helicopter products. The aircraft approaching isn't a Bell."

"How can you tell?"

"Different engines sound different." He put his finger to his lips to quiet her.

Outside, the chopper drew closer. It was flying low and approaching rapidly. A chill passed through Rachael when she remembered the way Bo's ranch house had exploded. Even though this house was built into the side of a hill, part of it was vulnerable.

Shaking off his grip, she started for the table, grabbed both her guns. She shoved the mini Magnum into her waistband and pulled back the slide on the Beretta, chambering a bullet. "I'm not going to stand here and become a s'more."

"They can't see us," Bo said.

She stopped midway to the door. "Can't infrared pick up our body heat?"

"We're beneath several tons of earth. The house is beneath the canopies of the cottonwood trees. They can't see heat through that." He motioned toward the door where full darkness was descending quickly. "You run out there and start shooting like some kind of hotheaded rookie and you'll do nothing but give away our location and give them a moving target."

"What about the shed row where the horses are?"

"Out of sight." His eyes met hers. "That's why we're here, Rachael. This place is hidden from the air."

It was then that she realized he'd kept this old place standing for just this purpose. Always have a plan B....

They listened to the chopper approach. Bo was standing so close, Rachael could smell his out-of-doors scent. He was still wearing his hat and his eyes were shadowed. But she knew he was watching her. She could feel the heat of his gaze on her skin.

Overhead, the chopper blasted past, but neither of them moved. She wanted to believe the pound of her heart was due to the danger that loomed so close. But she was honest enough with herself to admit her racing pulse had more to do with the man than the situation.

She listened to the sound of the engines fade into the night. Slowly, her surroundings came back into focus. The incessant chorus of crickets and frogs. The chill of the night pressing against her skin. The relief that came with danger narrowly averted.

But for the first time since she'd arrived at the Dripping Springs Ranch, Rachael realized she now faced another kind of danger. A danger that had nothing to do with Viktor Karas—and everything to do with the man who'd been hired to protect her.

Chapter Nine

"Close call," she whispered.

For a crazy instant Bo wasn't sure if she was referring to the chopper that had flown so low overhead or the strange moment that had just transpired between them.

He wanted to think the hard thrust of his heart was due to the ebb and flow of adrenaline in his blood, but he knew it had more to do with the close proximity of this woman.

Hands off, partner, a little voice warned.

Bo knew he should listen to that tiny voice of reason. He was far too level-headed to act on some reckless impulse. But God knew he wanted to.

It had been two years since he'd been with a woman, since he'd holed up at the

Dripping Springs Ranch and sealed himself off from the rest of the world. He spent more time with horses than he did with people. With the guilt churning in his gut, he had no use for friendships or relationships. He sure as hell didn't have a use for a woman.

But churning in his gut right alongside the guilt was something else that was every bit as powerful. A need so strong, all he could do was stand there, staring at her, and hope she didn't notice the fact that he was aroused.

The sound of the chopper's rotors had long since faded into the distance. Still, neither of them moved. Bo knew if he did move, it would be toward her. A mistake that would cost him what little peace of mind he had.

But he couldn't stop looking at her mouth. He couldn't stanch the need to pull her into his arms and get a taste of it.

If it hadn't been for his conscience reminding him who she was and what he'd done, he might've acted on the hot impulses streaking through him. But if Bo Ruskin was anything, he was cautious. He couldn't let himself put his hands on his best friend's wife…even if that friend had betrayed him.

Giving himself a hard mental shake, he stepped back. "I'm going to light the stove."

His hands were shaking when he reached for the canister and popped off the top. He used to have the steadiest hands of anyone he knew. He could set up a shot from two hundred yards away and hit his mark. But Rachael Armitage turned that steadiness into a bundle of raw nerves.

Shoving thoughts of her aside, he set the small camping stove on the table and lit the wick. Yellow light filled the kitchen. He could hear Rachael behind him, but he didn't turn around. For the first time in his life, Bo didn't trust himself. He wasn't sure what he'd do if he looked into her eyes. But he found himself wondering how she would react if he pulled her to him and pressed his mouth to hers….

"It's getting cold."

He actually started when she came up beside him. Feeling like a fool, he glared at her. "I brought a couple of blankets." He motioned to his saddlebag. "Help yourself."

She crossed to the table and pulled two blankets from the leather bag. "If Karas's men make another pass in the chopper, won't they see the light in the windows?"

If it were anyone but Viktor Karas looking for them, Bo would have pointed out that it would be counterproductive to fly a search mission at night. But he knew it was exactly the kind of thing Karas would do.

"Maybe." There were two windows and a door in the kitchen. Not a good place to keep the heater.

But in the adjoining living area there was only one large window. Picking up one of the blankets, Bo carried it to the living-room window and hung it on the rusty nails sticking out of the wood.

"You need that blanket for warmth, Bo."

"I'm not cold." It was a silly thing to say; of course, he was cold—or at least he would be by the end of the night. The temperature in the high country dropped to near freezing at night this time of year. Already, he could see his breath when he spoke.

Ignoring her as best he could, he went back to the kitchen, picked up the camping heater and carried it to the larger room. He set it on the floor in the center of the room, then sat down beside it.

After a moment, Rachael sat down across from him. She had the blanket wrapped around her shoulders. Yellow light flickered on her features. She was staring at the small ring of flame. All Bo could think was that she was one of the most beautiful women he'd ever seen in his life.

"You're shivering."

Her voice pulled him from his reverie. He hadn't noticed. "I guess I am."

Sighing, she scooted on her rear until she was next to him and lifted the blanket. "Put this over your shoulder. It'll help."

When Bo didn't budge, she scooted closer and draped the blanket over him. Then they were shoulder to shoulder; he could feel the warmth of her shoulder against his side. Her thigh brushed his, the sensation was warm and soft and forbidden. He closed his eyes against a quick rise of pleasure.

Logic and a healthy dose of self-preservation told him to keep his distance. All he had to do was go to the shed row where the horses were tied and bring in their saddle blankets. They wouldn't smell nearly as good as Rachael, but at least he wouldn't have to endure touching her.

Being this close to her—close enough to smell the wildflower scent of her hair— was enough to drive a man crazy. He wanted to blame it on two years of celibacy. But he knew it was more than that. Just as he knew it wouldn't take much for him to do something stupid. Like turn to her and take her mouth in a kiss....

Heat flared in his groin when she shifted and her thigh brushed against his hip. He felt every touch like the prod of a branding iron.

"I think the heater is taking the chill out of the room."

Bo swallowed. His throat was so tight the sound seemed to echo in the room. If he hadn't been so distracted, so off-kilter by the onslaught of sensations this woman induced, he might have laughed. Big, bad Bo Ruskin had finally met his match. But it hadn't come in the form of some gun-toting goon, but a woman half his size with pretty green eyes and a mouth he'd give his right hand for one taste...

"How long do you think it will be before the agency can send someone to pick us up?"

"I don't know."

She fell silent for a moment. Despite his distracted frame of mind, Bo could practically feel her brain working, churning out questions. "Any idea where Karas's goons have set up base? They need a place to set down that chopper."

"A lot of open country out here that's pretty desolate. A man could set down a chopper on the open range and not get noticed for days."

"So they could be anywhere." She turned slightly and looked at him.

Bo knew better than to meet her gaze. But he did anyway. In the yellow light from the heater, her eyes were level and dark. His gaze flicked to her mouth. Her lips looked soft and wet. Her face was only a few inches from his. All he had to do was lean forward....

Realizing he was one moment of bad judgment away from doing something he would regret the rest of his life, Bo pulled away. His heart was beating hard and fast in his chest when he scrambled to his feet.

Without speaking, he started toward the door.

"Bo?"

He knew better than to go outside. If the chopper happened by at that moment, the infrared would zoom in on the heat of his body and reveal their location. But he had to get out of there. Besides, it was quiet in the high country at night. Bo assured himself he would hear the engine and rotors coming from miles away.

The one thing he wasn't sure about was how he was going to get through the night trapped in a house with a woman he was attracted to beyond all logic.

A woman he could never have.

STARING INTO the heater's flame, Rachael huddled in the blanket and tried not to think of everything that had happened in the last twenty-four hours. Twenty minutes had passed since Bo walked out. She tried to convince herself he was only checking on the horses.

But she knew better.

He was avoiding her.

That was probably a good thing since there was so much electricity zinging between them. A fact that disturbed her nearly as much as the knowledge that Viktor Karas wanted her dead.

In the few scant minutes they'd been huddled together beneath the blanket, something powerful had been at work between them. Attraction. Affection. All the things she'd swore she'd never feel again after Michael. The feelings Bo elicited made her feel guilty. As if she were somehow betraying Michael. After all, Bo had been his best friend.

She was so much better at feeling nothing at all. Things were simpler that way. Easier.

Safer, a traitorous little voice added.

"Armitage, you are such an idiot," she muttered.

"Who are you talking to?"

She jumped at the sound of Bo's voice. Turning, she saw him silhouetted in the doorway of the kitchen. Wide shoulders. Narrow hips. Cowboy hat pulled low over his eyes.

"I didn't hear you come in," she said.

He pushed away from the jamb and approached her. "They always say talking to yourself is the first sign of insanity."

"If that's the case, I've been crazy for a long time."

He chuckled. "Me, too."

Rachael couldn't help it. She laughed. The tension between them lifted marginally. But she sensed Bo wanted to talk—a first since he was a man of few words. More than likely to tell her he was no more interested in some one-night tryst than she was. Thank goodness. After all, they were adults. Professional agents, for God's sake. They could handle whatever it was that was happening between them.

"Do you mind if I sit?"

She looked up at him as he approached. "I was hoping you would," she said.

He took his place on the opposite side of the small stove. Rachael noticed he'd brought in both of the wool horse blankets. Setting one on the ground, he draped the other over his shoulders and sat.

"Any sign of trouble outside?" she asked.

"Nothing."

"Hopefully, Karas will call off his dogs until daylight."

She figured they both knew that was a

best-case scenario. Viktor Karas wasn't known for giving up easily.

But the statement made her think of Cutter. Last they'd heard he'd been missing....

"I know using the cell phone isn't the smartest thing to do right now, but I'd like to call in and see what the status is on Cutter," she said.

The odds of Karas tracking a call were slim, but not impossible. All he'd have to do was have someone waiting at the phone company. From there they could do a triangulation trace and locate the cell tower.

"I'll make it quick." Bo tugged out his cell phone, then looked at her. "You want to listen?"

Getting any closer to him was a dangerous business; there were too many crazy impulses racing through her. But they were talking about the fate of a personal friend. A man they both cared for and respected.

She nodded. "Yeah."

"Scoot over here."

Rachael slid over until she was beside him. Bo hit two buttons, then put the phone to his ear and leaned toward her, close enough so she could hear.

The phone rang. She waited and listened, hoping against hope they would receive good news about Sean Cutter. The line clicked and the relay desk answered with a curt, "Headquarters."

"This is Alpha two-four-six," Rachael said.

A pause ensued while her ID code was verified.

"One moment," came the voice. Another click sounded while the call was transferred.

"This is Zero three-four-two."

Rachael sighed with relief at the sound of Mike Madrid's code number. Bo cut right to the point. "How's nine-nine-nine?" The code for Sean Cutter.

"No word. He's not in the rubble, though. At this point we can only assume he's been kidnapped."

Rachael heard each word like punch. She and Cutter hadn't always seen eye-to-eye on things—in fact, they'd disagreed on matters more often than not—but he was a good man and one of the best agents MIDNIGHT had. He was larger than life. The kind of man you turned to when you thought all was lost. To think of him at the mercy of a man like Viktor Karas sickened her.

"You got men on it?"

"All we can spare."

"What about other casualties?" Bo asked.

"Six-five-eight has a broken arm and some burns. I've got some minor lacerations. Compared to Cutter..." Madrid let his voice trail.

Six-five-eight was Jake Vanderpol. Rachael uttered a silent thanks that his injuries weren't life threatening. That none of her counterparts had been badly injured.

"What's the stat at headquarters?" Bo asked.

"You want the bad news or the bad news?"

Bo exhaled a curse. "Lay it on me."

"We lost our computers, Bo. From what I understand there's a backup system, a computer hub off-site where all data was dumped when we got hit. Everything we have, including surveillance, has been turned over to CIA. We can't guarantee security until we can get our sweepers working."

Sweepers was the term used for debugging communication systems, such as phones and computers.

Silence reigned as the information sank in. For the first time, Rachael felt alone—and vulnerable.

"What about Karas?"

"Last I heard we had a visual in Moscow. I haven't been able to check since we got hit."

"Why the hell is he just sitting there?" Bo asked.

"I don't know. But his presence was verified by a visual."

"We need a pickup," Bo said.

Madrid paused. "We're not secure, partner. Nine-nine-nine knows your twenty and he's not going to be talking for a while. Any way you can hang tight for a while?"

Now it was Bo's turn to pause. "Not for long."

"Let me make some calls. See what I can scramble. They're clearing me for a chopper at CIA. It's going to take a little while. You under direct fire?"

"Not yet, but it's only a matter of time."

Bo shook his head in frustration. "I can't stay on the line."

"Roger that. I'll call you back when I've got someone in the air. I'll need your coordinates at that time. In the interim, you're going to have to hang tight, buddy."

"Over and out." Bo snapped the phone closed and quickly turned it off. "Damn it."

Rachael caught a glimpse of uneasiness in his expression as he clipped the phone to his belt. "We're in trouble, aren't we?"

"We're on our own. Read into that what you want."

Sighing, she looked around, studying the darkened windows, half expecting a volley of rifle fire. "I've been in worse situations." She glanced at him. "I'm sure you have, too."

"Not like this." He shook his head as if in frustration. "I don't like this waiting. I don't like being outgunned. I sure as hell don't like being left without backup."

"If they approach via chopper, we'll hear them."

"Not if they put it down out of earshot and come for us on the ground."

Despite her efforts not to, Rachael shivered. That was the worst, she thought.

Not knowing where the enemy was. Not knowing how or when they would attack.

Bo must have felt her trembling because he put his arm around her. "I don't think they know where we are."

Rachael knew better than to take comfort in this man's arms. She was attracted to him in a way she hadn't been attracted to anyone since Michael's death. Attraction could be a dangerous thing. But she'd always been attracted to danger.

"It's only a matter of time before they figure that out," she whispered.

"This is a big ranch. It's surrounded by other big ranches," he said. "They have hundreds of acres to cover."

"Karas isn't stupid."

"No, but he's just a man. He doesn't have superhuman powers."

"Just big guns and lots of goons without consciences."

Dipping his head slightly, he turned her to him. When she didn't look at him, he put his fingers beneath her chin and forced her gaze to his. "I'm not going to let anything happen to you."

"You don't have to make me promises

like that. I know what we're up against. I know none of what's happening is within your control or mine."

"The only thing we can control is how we react. We're trained agents. We're armed. I know the lay of the land better than they do. If things get dicey here, I know where to go."

Because she didn't want him to know just how frightened she had become, she forced a smile. "You mean we have a plan B?"

"The creek bed we followed to this homestead is dry most of the year. But in the spring, heavy rains cause flash floods that have cut caves into the limestone walls. It's not the Ritz, but they'll do in a pinch."

"I reckon this qualifies as a pinch."

He smiled. "Did you just say 'reckon'?"

A tension-releasing laugh squeezed from her throat. "That was your line, wasn't it?"

"You've been spending too much time with this cowboy."

"I'm glad it's you," she said.

He looked away, as if her words made him uncomfortable. But he tightened his arm around her. "We're going to get out of this just fine," he whispered.

But Rachael figured they both knew he couldn't guarantee anything at this point. The only thing they knew for certain was that for now they were on their own.

Chapter Ten

Bo knew better than to get this close to her. He sure as hell knew better than to hold her. But the need ate at him like acid. Rachael Armitage was one of the most courageous women he'd ever met in his life. She was tough and willing to take on the world single-handedly if that's what it took to bring down her nemesis.

To see such a strong woman frightened to the point of trembling did something to him. Brought out the primal male need to protect. A dangerous business when there was so much physical chemistry between them. Add a hefty dose of adrenaline to the mix and he had a downright volatile situation on his hands.

But Bo had never been one to walk away from volatile.

Her eyes were as dark and luminous as the yellow glow of the stove's flame. Within their depths he saw all the things he didn't want to see. All the things he felt zinging around inside his own body. Fear. Adrenaline. A need that was as deep and mysterious as the night.

I'm glad it's you.

Her words echoed inside his head like the final notes of some sad ballad. He wondered how she would feel if she knew about Mike. If she would hate him when she found out the truth...

"I can't stop thinking about Cutter," she said after a moment.

"He's a strong man, both physically and mentally," Bo said. "If anyone can get through something like that, it's him."

"I used to think that about Michael."

The words went through him like a blade. Bo felt himself stiffen. His mind whirled with something to say, but there were no words. Just a deep, dark pit of guilt that churned with increasing velocity.

"I'm sorry," she said. "I don't know why I said that. I didn't mean to upset you."

"You didn't," he said a little too quickly, hating the defensive tone in his voice.

"I still think about him every day."

"Me, too."

She smiled, but he could see she was only trying to put him at ease. "You get into a situation like this and you can't help but think about your own mortality."

Bo didn't answer. He didn't want to think of mortality on a night when the reality of death loomed so threateningly near.

"I know you were there that night," she said. "I read it in the report."

"Yeah." His voice was rough, little more than a whisper.

"We haven't talked about it. I've been wanting to ask you about it." She shrugged. "The time never seemed right."

The time isn't right now, either, he thought. The time would never be right for him to tell her the truth about what happened. A truth not only about him, but about the man she'd loved. "It was a tough night," he said. "For all of us. I try not to think about it."

"But you do think about it, don't you?"

He turned away to stare at the darkened window and wished he was out there with the night, instead of inside with her and facing questions he did not want to answer. "Every day."

"If you don't want to talk about it, it's okay."

He looked at her, taken aback as much by her beauty as his reaction to her. He didn't want to know what it would be like to look into her eyes and see hatred reflected back at him. Even though he probably deserved it.

"What exactly do you want to know, Rachael? You read the reports." Reports that had been fabricated by Sean Cutter to protect other agents working undercover within Karas's organization "You know what went down."

"I mean, I know the mechanics of what happened that night. I looked at the reports the brass shared with me. But I've never had the courage to talk to anyone who was there." When he looked away, she reached out and touched his cheek with her hand, guiding his gaze back to hers. "I've seen my share of firefights, Bo. I know sometimes what appears on paper doesn't even begin to cover the realities of what really happened."

And sometimes what was on paper was an outright lie, he thought darkly. "Mike died a hero," he said thickly. "The rest of it doesn't matter."

Coward, a little voice accused.

"Did he screw up?" she asked. "Make a mistake? Or was he just at the wrong place at the wrong time?"

"Mike did what he had to do." Bo closed his eyes against the slash of pain that followed. *Go ahead. Tell her the truth, hotshot. Tell her you're the one who shot him. That you'd do it all over again if faced with the same situation.*

"I didn't mean to upset you."

"You didn't."

"Bo, you're shaking." She set her hand on his shoulder, but he shook it off.

"I'm fine, damn it."

"Or maybe what happened that night left more scars on more people than you're willing to admit."

He risked a look at her, wishing he could tell her the truth, just to get this crushing weight off his chest. But while the truth would set him free, he knew in the end she would hate him for it.

She was breathtakingly beautiful in the

yellow light from the fire. Looking into her eyes, he wondered what it would be like to touch her skin. He wondered what it would be like to lay her down and release the tension grinding inside him.

He envisioned himself leaning close and taking her lovely face between his hands. He imagined his lips touching hers. The taste of her mouth. The softness of her lips.

Temptation tugged him in one direction, guilt in another. But in the end the need to hold her was greater. Stronger than the need to do the right thing and walk away.

"You're playing with fire, Rachael."

"Bad habit of mine." She started to scoot away.

Reaching out, Bo stopped her. Then, taking her hand in his, he tugged her closer. She jolted when he set his palm against her face.

"You keep making me want you," he whispered. "What the hell am I supposed to do about that?"

"Don't do anything." But she leaned close and brushed her mouth against his.

The pleasure shocked his senses. The kiss was electric, her mouth everything he'd imagined and so much more. He drank in every sensation like a man dying of thirst. Soft, wet lips. A kiss so sweet and tender that for a moment all he could think of was taking her down on the floor and doing what he'd wanted to do since the moment he'd laid eyes on her.

A small voice of reason warned him that giving in to temptation was a mistake. But for the first time in what seemed like forever, Bo didn't listen to reason. All he heard was the call of lust heating his veins. The call of something else that was as deep and elusive as the night that embraced them.

Closing his eyes against the hot rush of lust, he shoved caution aside and reveled in the feel of this beautiful woman in his arms.

IT WASN'T OFTEN that Rachael surprised herself. But she certainly had when she'd kissed Bo. And then she got a hell of a lot more than she'd bargained for.

For a moment all she could do was absorb the pleasure kicking through her veins. All thoughts of Viktor Karas fled her mind and for a small space in time she and Bo were the only two people in the world. They were no longer agents, just a man and a woman caught up in the magic of desire.

They were sitting on the floor in front of the small camping stove, their bodies turned toward each other. Vaguely, she was aware of the hiss of butane as it burned. The nearly silent whisper of the wind outside the window. The call of an owl somewhere in the night.

Bo shifted closer and leaned into the kiss. Another layer of pleasure enveloped her when he put his arms around her and pushed her back. She could feel her heart beating like a drum in her chest. The roar of her pulse in her ears. Desire rose like a flashflood.

She didn't intend to let this continue. Rachael was far too smart—far too focused—to fall for something as banal as her hormones. But the feel of his mouth called to long-buried needs. She hadn't kissed a man since Michael. Never even wanted to until now. But she definitely wanted to kiss Bo.

Logic told her to pull away and get the situation under control. But when he moved over her and pressed his body to hers, the protest lodged in her throat transformed into a sound of acquiescence that slid between her lips like a sigh.

His body was lean and rock hard against hers. Somehow her arms had gone around him. She could feel him trembling against her, the steel shaft of his arousal pressing insistently against her belly.

He kissed her in a way that left no question that he was ready, willing and able to take this farther if she didn't put a stop to it now.

But the pleasure tore down her resistance. The razor-sharp edge of desire overrode her need for control. He ran his tongue along the seam of her lips. At the same time his hands slid from her face to her shoulders.

Turning his head slightly, he whispered, "Open to me."

The words came to her as if from a great distance. And even though logic ordered her to end this before things got out of hand, she opened to him.

His tongue slid between her teeth and went in deep. Rachael's control snapped. A wave of desire swamped her. She kissed him back, her tongue entwining with his as he explored her mouth. Good judgment and lust warred inside her. But she knew which would win.

His hands slid beneath the front of her jacket. With deft fingers he unfastened the buttons and opened it. For a moment the only sound came from the hard rush of their labored breathing.

Her mind spun out all the reasons why they shouldn't be doing this, the most obvious being the ruthless band of thugs who wanted them dead. But her body didn't care.

"I want to touch you," Bo whispered. "I've wanted to touch you since the moment I saw you."

He didn't wait for permission.

A groan squeezed from her throat when he set his hands over her breasts. All the while he kissed her senseless. Kissed her until she could think of nothing but easing the high-wire tension running through her body.

Sliding his hands beneath her sweatshirt, he brushed his fingers over her bra. A new and intense pleasure gripped her when his roughened fingers brushed over her sensitized nipples through the fabric. She arched, giving him full access.

He fumbled with the closure of her bra. Rachael gasped when the scrap of material opened.

"You're beautiful," Bo whispered.

For an instant she felt vulnerable and exposed. Then he lowered his mouth to her breast and all she felt was the contact of his lips against her skin.

She cried out when he suckled her, first one breast, then the other. The pleasure clamped down on her like a vise being turned ever tighter. She writhed beneath his ministrations. Her blood roared like a train in her ears. She could feel the blood pooling low in her body. The dampness between her legs.

She wasn't sure what pulled her back to reality. Perhaps the knowledge that at some point she'd relinquished her control. That she'd gone beyond the point of good judgment. Beyond logic. For the first time she heard the little voice in her head calling out for her to stop before things went too far. Before she did something irrevocable. Something she would be sorry for later.

In one smooth motion, she rolled out

from beneath him and scrambled to her feet. For several interminable seconds, she stood there staring at him, her breaths rushing out as if she'd just run a mile. Bo was sitting on the floor, looking as if he'd just wakened from some erotic dream. But his eyes were not sleepy. Even in the glow of the small heater, Rachael could see the undeniable heat of lust in them.

"I can't." The voice that squeezed from her throat sounded nothing like hers.

"It's all right." Bo's voice was just as foreign. "I shouldn't have—"

"Don't apologize," she said.

Never taking his eyes from hers, he got to his feet. He was looking at her the same way he'd looked at the frightened horse that day in the round pen. As if she were about to bolt.

It wasn't far from the truth. For the first time in a long time, Rachael wanted to run. Away from the emotions pounding her like waves. Away from the all the things he made her feel, made her want. Away from the man himself because she'd promised herself she would never feel again.

Spinning, she headed toward the back door. She heard him call out her name as she flung it open. But she didn't stop. Forgetting about the men who wanted her dead, she ran into the night toward the cover of the shed row.

Chapter Eleven

Bo shouldn't let her go. It wasn't safe for her to venture out. If Karas's men did a flyby at that moment—if the chopper was equipped with infrared—her body heat would stand out like a beacon and give away their position.

But because he didn't trust himself to keep his distance—because he was still painfully aroused—he stood his ground in the small living room and let her go.

"What the hell are you doing?" he muttered.

His voice was rough. To his surprise, he was still breathless. He could still feel the hot rush of blood through his veins. The pound of lust in his groin. But worse than the physical frustration was the knowledge that he'd screwed things up royally. He'd been hired to keep her safe from a group of criminals that wanted her dead. Not only was he on the verge of failing that, but he couldn't even muster the discipline to keep his hands off her.

"Better to let things cool off before you go running after her," he said aloud.

Scraping a hand over his unshaven jaw, he walked to the small kitchen and looked through the window at the darkness beyond and tried to school his thoughts into the mindset of the agent he'd once been. But he could no more conjure a logical thought than he could control his body. The truth of the matter was he wanted her. He wanted her more than he'd ever wanted a woman in his life.

But aside from his mission to keep her safe, there was also the problem of the truth. A truth he had yet to tell her. A truth that would bring an end to whatever it was that was happening between them.

"What a mess," he muttered.

He owed her an apology. For kissing her. For touching her when he should have been concentrating on keeping her safe. He owed it to himself to set things straight between them. More to the point, he needed to come clean about what happened two years ago.

Sighing, Bo left the house and headed toward the shed row. Around him, the night was cold and clear. The wind had kicked up, rustling the leaves of the cottonwood trees. A three quarter moon cast just enough light for him to find his way to the shed row without using the flashlight.

He found her with the horses, as he'd expected. She looked up when he entered the shed. Taking the tiny penlight from his jacket, he shone it on the ground to let her know he was approaching.

"Are you all right?" he asked.

Her gaze met his. Within the depths of her eyes he saw all the emotions he felt in his own heart. Regret. The remnants of a desire that could never be fulfilled. A guilt neither of them should feel, but did.

He crossed to her and stopped a safe distance away, watching as she caressed the muzzle of the Appaloosa. "I'm sorry," he said. "I was out of line. It was unprofessional and disrespectful. I shouldn't have let it happen."

"It's not like you did it all by yourself."

Bo couldn't help it. He laughed. Even visibly upset and caught in a terribly awkward position, she could come up with a pretty good one-liner. Damn it, not only was he attracted to her, but he *liked* her. A lot if he wanted to be honest about it. This was one of those situations when it was a lot simpler not to be quite so honest.

"I'm sorry I ran out like that," she said. "I know it was a stupid thing to do, especially with Karas's goons on the loose."

"I wasn't exactly behaving intelligently." Remembering the way she'd felt beneath him, he shifted his weight from one foot to the other. "Come back inside."

She hesitated. Bo motioned toward the house. "We need to get some rest. I wanted to talk to you about a contingency plan in case something happens tonight."

Her gaze snapped to his. "You think they'll be back?"

"Hard to tell with Karas. With this wind and the dark, I can't imagine any pilot flying a chopper. But then Karas is one of the most unpredictable sons of bitches I've ever had to deal with."

"Unless they don't use a chopper and approach us some other way," she offered.

"Whatever the scenario, we need to be prepared."

After a moment, she nodded and they started toward the house. The kitchen seemed warm and cozy compared to the drafty shed row, where the cold north wind whipped around the rafters and rattled the loose boards. Bo walked to the table and opened one of the saddlebags on the table. "I could use some coffee. You want a cup?"

Rachael stood at the sink, looking out the window. "Anything hot."

"I think I can handle that."

He poured water from the collapsible container into a small camping saucepan. Handing Rachael two tin cups, he took the pan and individual packets of coffee to the living room.

He set the pan on top of the stove and turned up the flame. Within minutes the water was boiling. Bo poured into the cups and handed one to Rachael.

She took the cup and sipped tentatively. "Not bad."

"I do okay in the coffee department. Just don't ask me to make toast."

She smiled, and Bo felt the tension

inside him ease just a little bit. Warning himself not to get off track again, he went back to the kitchen and pulled a map from the saddlebag and carried it into the living room.

"I thought I'd show you the location of the caves I was telling you about earlier." He sat down and spread the map on the floor between them.

"That's our contingency plan?"

"It's not brilliant, but the best I can come up with under the circumstances." Taking the penlight from his pocket, he shined it on the map where a big red star appeared. "This is the house here. The Dripping Springs Ranch is outlined in yellow Hi-liter."

She leaned closer. "Where are we?"

Setting down his coffee he pointed. "Here. The Dripping Spring Creek runs south from here, then curves slightly to the east. The caves are here, where the creek curves. The flood waters have eaten into the limestone, forming shallow caves that can't be seen from the air."

Bo risked a covert look at her. Her eyebrows knitted as she concentrated on the map. She was incredibly lovely in the yellow glow of the camping stove. He tried to keep his mind on the business at hand, but he couldn't stop thinking of the way she'd moved beneath him when he'd touched her. The softness and warmth of her flesh...

"What's the best way to get there from here?"

"Fastest way is to cut across the plain here." He slid his finger an inch lower. "But it's open country. The safest way is to follow the dry creek bed where there are trees for cover." He gave her a sober look. "There's something you need to know about those caves."

Her gaze latched on to his. "What?"

"I have explosives buried inside them."

She blinked, then a slow smile tugged at one side of her mouth. "That's one hell of a contingency plan. Why didn't you mention this sooner?"

"My mission is to keep you safe." He tapped the cave location on the map with his finger. "Not get into a war with Karas."

"You can take the man out of the agency, but you can't take the agent out of the man."

"Or maybe I just like to be careful."

"Why do you have the explosives?"

He sighed. "I'm a civilian now. But in the years I was an agent, I made some enemies. If they come looking for me, I want to be ready."

"Always have a plan B."

"I don't want any of my people at the ranch getting hurt because of me or my past."

She nodded, then turned her attention back to the map. "Tell me about the explosives."

"Give me your word you won't do anything stupid."

"Like what?"

"Like go after Karas yourself."

She met his gaze levelly. "That would be suicidal."

"And just your style." He didn't look away.

"So why are you telling me this if you feel you can't trust me?"

"If something happens to me, I want you to do what you need to do to survive. But I want your word that you won't do something crazy."

After a moment, she sighed. "All right. I won't go after Karas. Satisfied?"

Bo looked down at the map. Removing a pen from his jacket pocket, he made a small circle at a bend of the Dripping Spring Creek. "The caves are here. The explosives are buried in the middle cave, which is the largest. They're inside a watertight ammunition box beneath about a foot of sandy soil."

"What kind of explosives?"

"C-4. Dynamite. Nitro. Small arms. Ammo. Grenades."

She tossed him a startled look. "I guess you wanted to be prepared."

"Viktor Karas has a long memory."

"And he isn't exactly the forgiving type."

"To put it mildly."

Glancing uneasily over her shoulder at the darkened window, she huddled deeper in the blanket, then turned her gaze on Bo. "So what do we do now?"

"We wait. If the agency can't get a chopper to us, they may send local law enforcement."

"And in the meantime?"

He shrugged. "I suggest we bed down for the night. Get some rest."

"Hard to do when Viktor Karas wants both our heads on a platter."

He contemplated her, trying hard to see her as a capable and highly trained agent instead of a woman with pretty eyes and soft curves. But he failed miserably. "I'll keep first watch." He sighed. "If anything happens—"

"I know what to do."

When he only continued to stare at her, she added, "I've got pretty strong survival instincts."

"I know." But he sorely hoped she wouldn't have to rely on those instincts to survive the night.

RACHAEL LAY on the horse blanket and watched the yellow flame of the camping stove dance and hiss. Fifteen minutes ago, when Bo had suggested they get some rest, it had sounded like a good idea; the day had been stressful and physically grueling. But even though she was tired all the way to her bones, she couldn't turn off her mind.

She wanted to think she was keyed up because of the threat Viktor Karas posed. But she knew there was something much

more subtle—and every bit as dangerous—
hard at work deep inside her.

Every time she closed her eyes, her mind
took her back to the intimacies she and Bo
had shared earlier. Her response to him
troubled her. Rachael was no stranger to
desire; she'd been married for two years to
a man she was very much in love with.
After his death, that part of her had shut
down. In the two years since his death,
she'd felt nothing. She hadn't *wanted* to
feel anything. And she hadn't missed it.

Then along came Bo Ruskin with his
slow drawl and soft touch, and all the
needs she'd refused to feel for two long
years came rushing back with a vengeance.
Damn him for making her feel again.
For making her want. Both were complica-
tions she didn't want to deal with. Not
now. Not ever.

But there were other factors at play that
added to her resolve to stay away from Bo.
As much as she didn't want to admit it, fear
was a big part of it. The fear of getting too
close again. The fear that she would
somehow be betraying Michael. The fear
that she would lose control of emotions
she swore she'd never relinquish again.

Losing Michael had been the most difficult ordeal she'd ever been through in her life. She'd loved him with all her heart and soul. For two years she'd believed the part of her that was capable of love had died the night he was killed.

Love?

The thought startled her, made her break a sweat even though the house was chilly. It was absurd to think she was falling in love with Bo. All they'd shared was a kiss and a touch, neither of which equated love. Still, Rachael could no longer deny she felt something powerful and real for the former MIDNIGHT agent. She preferred to think it was the reawakening of her hormones after a long hiatus. Simple and basic human need. She could deal with that. What she couldn't deal with was the reality that there was a whole lot more to her feelings for Bo than she was admitting.

"Can't sleep?"

She looked up to see him standing in the kitchen doorway, holding one of the saddles by its horn.

"I didn't mean to startle you," he said.

"You didn't." Propping herself up on her elbows, she watched him cross to the heater and set the saddle on the floor. "I thought this might make you more comfortable," he said referring to the saddle.

"I'm fine," she said.

"Suit yourself." He shifted the saddle, then sat down and propped his head against the soft leather seat so that he was partially reclined. He'd removed his hat at some point. It was too dark for her to make out the details of his face, but she could tell he was watching her.

"You got something on your mind?" Giving up on the idea of sleep, Rachael sat up.

"It's about the night Michael died."

For two years she'd tried—and failed—not to dwell on that terrible night. But she'd always wanted to know more about her husband's final moments. If he'd been frightened. If it had happened quickly. If he'd thought of her...

"Okay." But at some point her heart had begun to pound. She got a bad feeling in her gut. A feeling that told her he was about to tell her something she didn't know. Something she hadn't anticipated.

For a moment the only sound came from the whistle of the wind outside. Somewhere in the distance a great horned owl screeched.

"Mike and I had been trying to nail Viktor Karas for two years," he began. "When we finally decided how to do it, we spent another six months choreographing the sting. We knew what to do. We knew Karas would bite. We took a bunch of confiscated weapons from federal evidence and set up shop in a warehouse. They were exactly the kind of weapons Karas had been looking for to resell to whomever was planning a war. Rocket launchers. Grenades. Military-type explosives, including C-4. But it was the plutonium he really wanted."

Shock vibrated through her. She hadn't known about the plutonium. None of the reports she'd read had mentioned it. Cutter hadn't mentioned it. Neither had Michael....

"I didn't know," she said, amazed by the revelation.

"Karas was planning something big," Bo continued. "We had the weapons. He had the money. Everything was going as planned. Karas showed right on schedule. We had backup in place. But before the deal could go down and our guys could move in, he made us as federal agents. We didn't know how it had happened at the time—"

"Karas tortured an agent stationed in Moscow," she offered. "I read it in the report. After six hours, he talked. I don't begrudge any agent talking under those circumstances."

Bo looked away, his jaw clamped tight. Rachael watched him, wondering if he was going to throw something else at her she hadn't known. Until this moment she'd taken the agency's reports as gospel.

"There was no agent in Moscow," he said.

"But why would the reports and Cutter tell me there was?"

"Because there was more going on than you were ever privy to."

"Like what?"

"Like the fact that Mike was killed by one of our own."

"Bo, I know it was friendly fire." That was one of the reasons she'd always blamed his death on Karas. If the kingpin hadn't been running weapons, none of what happened that night would have taken place. As a result she'd spent the last two years trying to bring the son of a bitch to justice. She owed Michael that much.

The beep of a cell phone made both of them jump. For a moment she was so focused on Bo, on what she was about to say, that she didn't realize it was hers.

His gaze locked with hers. "Who is it?"

She fumbled to unclip the phone from her belt and flipped it open. Her heart surged when she read the display. "It's Cutter."

He nodded, and she hit Talk. "This is Alpha two-four-six," she said, using her code.

"Hello, Rachael."

The hairs at her nape stood on end at the sound of Viktor Karas's voice. It was so unexpected that for an instant she was speechless. Then her training kicked in. She mouthed, "Karas," and motioned for Bo to slide over and listen.

"Keep it short," he whispered. "He's trying to get a triangulation started on the cell tower."

But Karas was already speaking. "How

do you like being the mouse instead of the cat?"

"Tell me where you are and I'll answer that in person," she said evenly.

"Ah, Ms. Armitage, you never cease to entertain."

"Enjoy it while you can because you are about to take a very big fall."

His cultured laugh flowed through the line like rich red wine. "You Americans. So brash. So bold. You put way too much emphasis on those John Wayne heroics." His voice lowered, turned ominous. "Speaking of John Wayne, I hope you're getting on well with Bo Ruskin. Are you enjoying your stay at Dripping Springs Ranch?"

The words—the fact that he'd just verified knowledge of their location—jangled her nerves, but her voice didn't betray her. "If you know where I am, why don't you come get me?"

"In due time."

"I would apologize for the loss of your men, but then you don't mind collateral damage, even in your own camp, do you?"

"Merely the cost of doing business."

Vaguely, she was aware of Bo speaking

to her in a low tone, but she couldn't make out his words over the hard pounding of her heart. "Where's Cutter?"

Karas ignored the question. "Last time we spoke, I promised you the truth about your dearly departed husband, remember?"

She'd sworn she wasn't going to let Karas yank her chain. The one thing she could not do was let this get personal. But the mention of Michael made her hand tighten on the phone. "You don't know anything about him."

"Or maybe you're afraid to hear the truth."

"I'm not afraid of anything, including you because I'm going to take you down."

Beside her, Bo tapped his watch. "Time's up," he said. "Disconnect."

"You better have a deep hole to crawl into, Karas, because we're coming for you," she said.

"I look forward to it, Ms. Armitage. Rest assured, it won't be long."

Wresting the phone from her hand, Bo hit the End button.

Rachael spun on him. "What are you doing?"

"Keeping you from getting careless."

Bo was right; she knew better than to engage Viktor Karas in a lengthy phone conversation. But her need to bring him down overrode good judgment.

"Don't let him get to you like that," Bo snapped. "That's what he wants. Why do you think he called?"

Frustrated, feeling like a greenhorn fool, she spun away and paced the length of the living room. "I hate this," she said. "Sitting here. Trapped. Doing nothing while that son of a bitch plays with us."

"His day is coming."

"His day should have been here a long time ago."

"Calm down."

"Don't tell me to calm down." Impotence boiled inside her, like a wound that had been left to fester for two long and unbearable years. "Calm isn't going to get the job done."

"It's going to keep us alive."

She barely heard the words; she certainly didn't hear the wisdom they held. "Cutter had no right to pull me off the operation. I'd put two years of hard work into it."

"Cutter did the right thing and you know it."

"I was close. Too close to pull."

"You were close to getting yourself killed. Cutter recognized that and stopped it."

Anger joined the chorus of emotions singing through her. "I'm tired of playing it safe." She crossed the room again, stopping at the old hearth and slapping her hand against the ancient brick. "*Damn* it."

She jolted when strong hands landed on her shoulders. She hadn't heard him cross to her. She certainly hadn't expected him to touch her.

"You're shaking," he said.

"I'm tired of sitting around and waiting for that bastard to strike again."

"We don't have a choice but to wait this out."

"Yes, we do." Shaking off his hands, she turned to him. "We could go on the offensive."

"You don't even know where he is."

"I don't have to know because we both know he'll come to me. I'm the one he wants. I killed his son. Don't tell me that's not the best way to smoke the rat out of his hole."

"You going to do that all by yourself, huh?"

"I can and you know it."

Bo shot her a dark look. "You're acting like some hotheaded rookie."

"I'm acting like an agent who refuses to be intimidated and knows how to get the job done."

His expression exuded anger when he moved closer. His mouth went taut when he set his hands on her shoulders and gave her a shake. "Don't get crazy on me, Rachael. I know you want him. So do I. But we can't do this on our own. Don't give him the chance to take another life."

Her anger boiled over. "My life means nothing as long as he's alive."

"You're blinded by revenge."

"He killed my husband!" she shouted, pulling away.

"Mike died because he made a mistake."

"Karas is indirectly responsible. He pulled out all the stops. He tortured agents for information that blew Mike's cover. How much more damage are we going to let him do before we stop playing by the rules?"

Only then did she realize she was crying.

She hated the display of weakness. Credibility and competence were important to her. Yet here she was, choking back sobs like some teenager who hadn't gotten her way.

"Those rules are what separates us from men like Karas," Bo said. "Don't let him blur those lines for you, Rachael. You're above that."

"No, I'm not." Frustrated with herself, she choked back a sob and wiped frantically at the tears. "It's what we do at the MIDNIGHT Agency, Bo. We blur lines. We cross lines. We do it because we know sometimes that's what it takes to win."

"Not like this."

"He's winning, damn it."

He started toward her. Rachael knew what would happen next, and she dreaded it with every fiber of her heart. But there was a small treacherous part of her that at that moment wanted Bo to touch her.

"Don't," she said.

"Too late."

His arms went around her. She resisted the pull to him. Her body went rigid. She shoved against his chest. But he was like a stone wall against her, solid and strong and impenetrable. But the heady sensation of his arms going around her tore down her resistance piece by ragged piece. Pleasure teased her senses. His scent filled her nostrils, titillated her brain.

"Easy," he said.

Rachael sank into the solid warmth of him. She absorbed his essence like dry earth absorbing rain after a long and killing draught.

The emotional dam broke with a surge she hadn't experienced since the night Sean Cutter knocked on her door in the middle of the night and told her Michael was dead.

Setting her head on Bo's shoulder, she cried openly. She cried so hard her body shook with the power of it. All the while, he held her. He stroked her, murmuring gentle words. The same way he'd calmed the young horse the other day.

"It's going to be all right," he whispered. "I know it doesn't seem that way at the moment. But I promise you'll get through this. We'll get Karas. But not tonight."

Pulling back slightly, she looked into his

eyes. "How many more people have to die before that happens?"

"I can't answer that because I don't know. All I can tell you is that you're safe here with me. Once the agency is up and running, they'll go after him no-holds-barred."

"I wanted to be the one," she choked.

"You did your part. You did everything you could. Now it's time for you to step aside and let someone else continue on with your work."

Embarrassed by her outburst, she wiped at the tears on her cheeks with the sleeve of her jacket. "I'm not very good at stepping aside."

"Now there's a revelation." Setting his fingers against her cheek, he wiped at a tear with his thumb. "Don't cry."

"I've been telling myself that for the last couple of minutes and it's not working."

He smiled. "You had a lot bottled up inside you."

"I'm a sore loser."

"We haven't lost this yet."

He was looking at her intently. His body was flush against hers. Surprise and something akin to alarm went through her when she realized he was shaking. And for the first time she realized the moment had become intimate. That she wasn't the only one who'd noticed.

She knew he was going to kiss her an instant before he moved. A keen sense of self-preservation ordered her to stop him. She was feeling vulnerable and damningly needy—not a good state of mind in which to be partaking in something as dangerous as a kiss from Bo Ruskin. But the part of her that was a woman first—a woman who'd been alone for a very long time— didn't want to stop what she knew would happen next.

His mouth came down on hers with the awesome power of a thunderstorm, pounding rain onto a parched ground. Rachael soaked in the quick shock of pleasure. She closed her eyes against the quick slice of heat when his tongue slid between her lips and went deep.

His body moved against hers. She got the impression of a hard as granite chest. Powerful arms that trembled with restraint. Chiseled lips that knew how to tear down a woman's resistance.

Two years of loneliness and pain and self-denial rose in a dangerous tide. Every nerve in her body went taut. Physical yearning warred with the more intellectual need to stop the madness. But all she could think of was one more kiss....

Cupping the back of her head, he deepened the kiss. It was raw and primal and seemed to suck the breath right out of her lungs. She could feel her heart laboring beneath her ribs. Her blood roared like a freight train in her ears. Growling, he moved against her. The steel rod of his erection nudged her belly.

"I know it's wrong, but I want you," he whispered.

"I've always had problems with rules."

Pulling back just enough to make eye contact, he smiled. But the moment of levity was short-lived. She saw stark need in his eyes. The knowledge that they were about to cross a line that couldn't be traversed a second time.

Rachael didn't care. She kissed him back with a recklessness that shocked her. His hands went to her breasts. A shudder rippled through her when he brushed his hands over the fabric. Her breasts grew heavy and full. Her nipples ached with the need for the warm wetness of his mouth.

He opened her jacket with trembling hands and lifted her sweatshirt. A clever flick of his wrist and the front closer of her bra opened. He dipped his head and took her nipple into his mouth.

Her control broke with the violence of a chain snapping under tremendous pressure. Throwing her head back, she went wild in his arms. Her body writhed against his. An urgency she'd never felt before burned her, like a fire had been ignited somewhere deep inside her and only Bo's touch could douse it.

"Easy," he whispered.

But Rachael was beyond comprehension. Beyond speech. And far beyond thinking. At the moment, all she could do was soak in the pleasure Bo was giving her.

Sweeping her into his arms, he carried her to the blanket near the heater. Kneeling, he laid her down. Rachael caught a glimpse of his eyes. Intensity burned within the depths of his gaze. No man had ever looked at her that way. As if she were the only woman in the world and this was their last moment together. An instant of pain pierced her heart when it struck her that not even Michael had looked at her like that. But the moment of cognizance was fleeting.

Gently, he pushed her back, and came down on top of her. Her thought processes short-circuited when his mouth swooped down on hers. The rest of the world ceased to exist when he came full length against her. The power of the emotions churning inside her stunned her. She'd forgotten what it felt like to be held by a man. She knew she was vulnerable, still recovering from the loss of a man she'd planned to spend the rest of her life with.

But Bo Ruskin was warm and strong and alive. He was here and he wanted her. He represented life when, for the last two years, too much of Rachael's life had evolved around death and a past that was lost.

Somehow she managed to get her arms out of her jacket. Sitting up, Bo reached for the hem of her sweatshirt and drew it over her head. Cold air rushed over her sensitized breasts. Her nipples went hard. Her breasts ached. He reached for the band in her hair and slid it off. His eyes glittered when her hair cascaded to her neck.

"You're beautiful," he said.

The words embarrassed her; Rachael didn't think she was beautiful. But he made her feel that way. For now, it was enough.

He sat back on his heels and worked off his jacket. Feeling awkward, needing to do something, Rachael reached for the buttons on his shirt and was shocked to see her hands shaking violently.

Noticing them, Bo took her hands into his. "You're shaking." He brought her hand to his mouth and brushed a kiss to her palm. "Your hands are cold."

"I have a really warm heart."

He ducked his head to make eye contact and smiled at her. "Are you okay with this?"

She smiled back. "I'd be really disappointed if we stopped now."

Leaning close he brushed his mouth against hers. "I think I'd die right here and now."

"Coroner would have a hell of a time with the cause of death."

He threw his head back and laughed.

She joined him and for a moment the sound of simple human joy filled the rooms of the old homestead.

Rachael finished with the buttons on his shirt. Bo tossed it aside. She couldn't stop looking at his chest. His pectoral muscles were rounded and covered with a thin layer of black hair that tapered to his navel and then disappeared into the waistband of his jeans. She didn't even realize she was going to touch him until her fingertips brushed his skin. A tremor went through him when she ran her fingers over his nipples, taking in the rock hard feel of him. The muscles beneath her palms quivered with unleashed power.

"I've wanted you to touch me like that for a long time," he said in a tight voice.

Suddenly overcome with emotion and the enormity of what they were about to do, Rachael surprised herself by blinking back tears. "This is the first time I've...I mean, since Michael..."

"I know." He kissed her then. Not with the wild abandon of before, but a gentle touching of mouths that assured her everything was going to be all right. For the first time in a long time, she believed it.

He pulled away and his hands went to the button of her jeans. Rachael's heart beat out of control when he unfastened them and gently shoved them down her hips until she wore only her panties.

"Lie down," he said.

She lay down on the horse blanket. He covered her with the softer camping blanket. Desire pounded through her as she watched him remove his own jeans. Her body felt electric when he finally slid beneath the blanket beside her. His body was like warm, smooth stone against hers. She swept her fingers over his chest and abdomen and was surprised all over again when he trembled against her.

"I'm not the only one shaking," she whispered.

He smiled at her, but his eyes were tense. "My secret's out."

"What secret is that?"

Moving quickly, he took her face between his hands and looked deeply into her eyes. "This is scaring the hell out of me. I've never felt this way before. Ever."

She wanted to tell him it was the same for her. But the power of the moment stole her voice. Took her breath away. But it was then she realized she didn't have to say anything at all.

He kissed her deeply. Rachael threw her head back and absorbed his kisses. She cried out when he entered her. His name burst from her lips when he brought her to climax. She could feel her body gripping his when he went rigid and spilled his seed into her.

For the span of several seconds all she could do was absorb everything that had happened between them. The magic. The emotion. The physical sensation of being so close to another. Then he lowered his mouth to hers and the rest of the world faded away.

Chapter Twelve

Bo leaned his head against the leather seat of the saddle and listened to Rachael's rhythmic breathing. They'd made love twice and then she'd fallen into a deep sleep, evidently brought on by total exhaustion. He was exhausted himself, if he wanted to be honest about it. But his mind was troubled, and he knew sleep would not come. He couldn't stop thinking about what he'd done. The rightness of being with her warred with the wrongness of the secrets festering inside him. And it ate at his peace of mind, like acid at steel.

This is the first time... since Michael...

Her words rang uncomfortably in his head. He'd known she hadn't moved on since losing Mike. The knowledge hadn't been enough to keep him away. He couldn't help but wonder how she would feel if she knew it had been *his* bullet that ended her husband's life. That it hadn't been an accident.

Being with her like this was one of the most erotic experiences of his life. Making love to her had touched him in places he'd long since forgotten even existed. She'd reminded him what it was like to be a man. What it was like to be a human being. She'd reminded him that life wasn't just about pain and retribution, but joy and pleasure, too.

He stared into the darkness, his mind and heart in turmoil, his body already wanting her again. He couldn't believe he'd done the one thing he'd sworn he wouldn't. She'd been vulnerable, in the process of healing. He hadn't cared. He'd wanted her so much he'd been willing to sell his soul for just one night with her, and he hated himself for it.

Sleeping with her wasn't the worst of what he'd done. The worst of it was that he'd slept with her without first telling her the truth about what happened that night. He wasn't sure he could handle looking into her eyes and seeing betrayal—or worse, seeing hatred. That wasn't to say he didn't deserve either of those things. Maybe he did. The only question that remained was what he was going to do about it.

"If I didn't know better, I'd think you were having second thoughts about what just happened."

He glanced at her just as she snuggled close and put her head on his shoulder. "I thought you were sleeping," he said.

"I was."

She was incredibly warm and soft against him. Despite his resolve not to dig this hole he was in any deeper, he put his arm around her and pulled her even closer.

"Are you?" she asked.

He didn't know what to say. Didn't know what to feel. The only thing he knew for certain was that he owed her the truth even if that truth was going to shatter what they had.

"I'm…troubled."

"By what just happened?"

"Not that," he said. "Never that."

Looking concerned, she propped herself up on an elbow and looked into her eyes. "Then what?"

He closed his eyes briefly, then turned to her and met her gaze. "What we just shared was one of the most incredible experiences of my life."

She smiled, but he saw the presence of nerves and knew he was the cause. "Me, too," she admitted. "It's been a while. I'm a little out of practice."

"No, you're not."

"But?"

He took a deep breath, surprised when it wasn't quite steady. "I haven't been honest with you about something."

Her eyes went wary. "In what way?"

"I know something about Mike that I haven't told you," he said. "Something that was never made public."

"What are you talking about?"

"I'm talking about what happened that night."

"I know what happened."

"No, you don't."

"You're scaring me, Bo."

"I'm sorry. I don't mean to. But... I need to tell you everything." When she said nothing, just looked at him with new caution in her eyes, he sighed. "Mike and I engineered the entire sting. We worked on it for months before putting everything into play that night."

"I know something went wrong. I know you and Michael were involved in a firefight. I know he got into the wrong position, into the line of fire—"

"It didn't happen the way you think. The way it's written in the reports."

For the first time fear entered her expression. Fear because she knew he was about to throw something at her she wasn't prepared to handle. "But—"

Because he couldn't prolong the inevitable any longer, Bo cut her off. "I have to preface by saying he was a good man, Rachael. A good agent. And I loved him like a brother."

He took a deep breath, but it didn't keep his heart from pounding hard in his chest, his pulse from racing. "Mike wasn't killed by friendly fire."

She blinked. "But that's what I was told from the very beginning. Cutter and the reports stated as much."

Aching inside, he looked into her eyes. "It was me who fired the killing shot. And it wasn't an accident, Rachael. I shot and killed him because he was working for Karas."

RACHAEL HEARD THE WORDS as if from a great distance, even though he was so close she could feel the heat of his body against the length of hers. But as the words sank into a brain that didn't want to believe, warmth turned to ice.

In one smooth motion, she sat up, taking the blanket with her and holding it to cover herself. Shock and disbelief and a thousand other emotions she couldn't begin to name churned inside her. "I don't believe you."

Bo held her gaze. "Mike turned on me that night, Rachael."

The words hit her with the violence of a boxer's punch. Rachael felt herself recoil. Dread and a keen sense of betrayal dropped into her gut like a chunk of ice.

"He wouldn't," she heard herself say. "Michael was loyal to the agency."

"I don't know why or how he was being coerced, but he was working for Karas."

"No. You're wrong. I would have

known. Cutter would have told me, damn it."

"Cutter couldn't say anything without blowing the entire operation."

"You're lying. I was part of the operation. I knew what was going on."

"You didn't know all of it."

Rachael felt as if he'd just thrown a bucket of ice water in her face. Losing Michael had been the worst thing she'd ever endured in her life. For two years she'd believed Viktor Karas was responsible, at least indirectly. She'd dedicated her life to hunting him down and bringing him to justice. Finding out Michael had been working for the wrong side was like a knife in the back. She'd been lied to. Betrayed by the man she loved. By the agency she'd trusted with her life. By the man she'd just given her heart and soul to.

She stared at Bo, a terrible, burgeoning agony rising inside her. The blood rushing through her veins roared like a white water rapid. She could feel her heart crashing against her ribs. Her breaths rushing short and fast from between clenched teeth.

Because she didn't want this man to see

just how close she was to coming apart at the seams, she turned away and slipped quickly into her clothes.

"Rachael?"

"Stay away from me." She rose on unsteady legs and walked to her saddlebag. Her knees shook so violently she thought they might buckle. But they didn't. Like a hundred other times in the last two years, they held when she felt like collapsing into a broken heap. She would get through this. Just like she'd gotten through everything else.

"I'm sorry, Rachael. I'm so damn sorry. It was a terrible time for all of us. One I've relived a thousand times."

"I don't believe you." Rising, she walked to the kitchen. She found her backpack and reached into it for what she needed.

Stepping quickly into his jeans, he followed her as far as the kitchen door. She turned to face him. Pain twisted inside her when she looked into his eyes. The pain etched into his every feature was as evident as the pain running through ever fiber of her own heart.

But all the pain in the world wouldn't bring back Michael or preserve the memory of him she'd held close since his death.

Bo wasn't wearing a shirt, but she didn't let her gaze drop to his chest. She didn't let herself admire the sleek male muscle or the thatch of dark hair that tapered to a washboard belly. The belly she'd caressed just minutes before. The memory of what it had felt like to love him broke her heart.

"I wish there was some way I could change what happened that night," he said. "But I can't. It's done. Mike was a double agent."

"There's no way he was working for Karas," she said in a shaking voice. "He hated him."

"He could have been under duress. Karas could have threatened him in some way, forced him to cooperate. We don't know."

"Why didn't Cutter tell me? Why wasn't I briefed, damn it?"

"Cutter did what he could to protect Mike's memory, hence the friendly-fire report. Plus, he couldn't let Karas know we were on to him, so he let everyone believe it had been a friendly-fire incident."

"You're lying."

"You know I'm not." Bo stared at her as if he were trying to solve some complex puzzle that refused to come together. "I wanted to tell you a hundred times."

"Instead, you ran away and spent the last two years hiding out at this ranch."

He looked away. "Something like that."

Fresh anger coursed through her at the thought of how she'd been duped. By Sean Cutter. By Bo Ruskin. By the agency she'd devoted her entire adult life to.

Why, Michael?

"Rachael, you need to trust me on this. You know I'd never say anything to hurt you."

"You already did. You slept with me, and then you lay this on me, you bastard."

"I didn't mean for it to happen that way."

"You should have told me...before. It would have changed everything."

"Would it?"

"Yes, damn it! I wouldn't have—"

Anger entered his expression. "You know as well as I do that something happened between us. Something we didn't expect. Something good and right that was meant to be whether you want to admit it or not."

She wouldn't admit it, but he was

right. They'd made magic tonight. Magic that had been healing and powerful and totally unexpected. Still, Rachael clung to her anger. It was all she had now. The only thing that was going to get her through this.

"You think Karas coerced him?" she asked.

"That's exactly what I think."

"That would have killed him inside," she said.

"I know."

"How could Karas coerce him?"

He shrugged. "Karas could have threatened you. We'll probably never know."

Closing her eyes briefly, she gathered her resolve and struggled to pull herself together. Put her thoughts into order. She knew what she had to do. Not for Michael. Not for Bo or Sean Cutter or even the agency. But for herself.

She raised her eyes to Bo's and said the words that would put her plan into motion. "I'm sorry I went off on you like that."

"You're entitled. I'm just sorry I had to tell you. I never wanted to hurt you."

"That's why you haven't been able to pick up your weapon."

He didn't meet her gaze. "I developed hoplophobia after the shooting. Fear of firearms."

"I'm sorry."

"Don't be. I'm handling it."

The tears came without effort. "Do you think you could just hold me for a moment?"

He blinked at her as if her words had surprised him. His expression turned uncertain. Never taking his eyes from hers, he crossed to her. But Rachael couldn't meet his gaze. She couldn't look into his eyes knowing what she had to do next.

His arms went gently around her and she fell against him. His body was warm and solid and incredibly reassuring against hers.

Closing her eyes, Rachael raised the syringe. "I'm sorry, Bo."

"You have nothing to be sorry—"

She jabbed the needle deeply into his neck and depressed the plunger with her thumb. Reeling backward, he reached up and cupped the injection site. "What the hell did you do?"

Rachael tossed the spent syringe onto the floor. "It's styezipam."

Styezipam was a fast-acting tranquilizer many of the MIDNIGHT agents carried. In all the years Rachael had been with the agency, she'd never had to use it. It was the ultimate irony that the one and only time she called upon it, she would use it on a fellow agent.

Bo's expression went from regret, to shock, to anger. "Rachael, for God's sake, what are you doing?"

"What I should have done a long time ago."

He gripped his neck as if trying to keep the drug from leaching into his bloodstream. "Don't do anything stupid."

"The only stupid thing I've done lately is sleep with you." Even though she was furious with Bo for not being truthful with her, the words didn't ring true.

"It meant something to me, damn it." He stepped toward her.

She stepped back. Though the drug was fast-acting—usually within four to seven minutes—it hadn't yet taken effect. She would have to be careful because she knew he would try to stop her.

He took another step toward her. "Stay away from Karas."

"Keep your distance, Bo. You can't stop me."

"I'm not going to let you get yourself killed." He started toward her at a determined clip.

Rachael backed toward the door. If he got too close she could escape and run to the barn. There was no way he could make it all the way out there before the tranquilizer slowed him down.

She was right.

At the table, Bo staggered and leaned heavily against it. Blinking at her, he shook his head as if trying to regain his equilibrium. He lifted his arm as if to reach out to her. "Don't do this," he said. "Please."

"I have to."

He lunged at her, but Rachael stepped quickly back. His knees buckled and hit the floor with a thud, but he didn't go down. Instead, he stayed on his knees, swaying, staring at her as if his lack of physical mobility stunned him. The truth of the emotions she saw in his eyes twisted her heart into knots.

"Don't go." His words slurred. He tried

to move toward her on his knees, but fell forward onto the floor. Rachael hated seeing him immobile, hated it even more than she'd had to resort to drugging him.

"I'm sorry, Bo," she whispered and slipped out the door and into the night.

Chapter Thirteen

Bo fought the drug, but he knew from experience the powerful tranquilizer would win. He'd administered it himself in the course of his career too many times to have any doubts about its effectiveness. Because he'd had to leave the ranch so suddenly, he hadn't brought along the antidote that would counteract the drug. Now he had no choice but to ride it out.

Not an easy chore when the woman he loved was about to get herself killed.

Loved?

The thought startled him. He wanted to blame it on the effects of the drug or high emotions left over from a night of love-making. But Bo knew his feelings for Rachael had nothing to do with the tranquilizer—and everything to do with his heart.

"Damn crazy woman."

Rolling onto his side, he squinted at his watch. Alarm shot through him when he realized he'd been out for over an hour. Styezipam was fast acting, but its effects were short lived.

Struggling to his feet, he swayed and looked around. The room tilted once, then leveled off. He blinked against a swirl of dizziness, then staggered to the kitchen.

"Rachael!" he shouted. *"Rachael!"*

But he knew she was gone.

Grabbing the remaining saddlebag from the table, he stumbled back into the living room. One saddle and blanket lay on the floor; she must have taken the other. Dread curdled in his gut when he realized she'd probably taken one of the horses as well. "Damn. Damn. Damn!" he snarled.

He scooped up saddle and blanket and headed out the door. Burdened with the tack, dizzy from the aftereffects of the tranquilizer, he ran awkwardly to the shed row.

Worst-case scenario became a reality when he found only one horse in the shed row. Rachael was not an expert horsewoman; he couldn't believe she'd taken off on horseback. But considering her frame of mind and the ugly truth he'd thrown at her, he knew she was capable of anything, including going after Viktor Karas.

The only question that remained was whether or not he was going to be able to stop her before it was too late.

Holding that terrible thought, he tacked up the horse, tied on the saddlebags, shoved the rifle into its sheath and rode into the night.

LIGHTNING FLASHED through the canopies of the pinion pines and cottonwood trees as the horse made its way along the dry creek bed. Wind from the approaching storm sent dry leaves skittering along the sandy banks. The yellow grass of the plain beyond whispered like the ghosts of some long dead pioneers.

Rachael would have preferred a different mode of travel. Not only was she a terrible rider, but the horse was injured. Though the gunshot wound was not life threatening and the animal wasn't limping, she worried that he was in pain. But the horse was all she had; she was going to have to make do. The weather wasn't helping matters. Several times the horse had danced when lightning speared the sky and thunder rumbled like the approaching footsteps of some massive beast.

Reaching down, she patted the animal's shoulder, hoping he would get her to the cave without mishap—and long before Bo regained consciousness and came after her.

She'd considered leaving him without a horse. But with Viktor Karas and his thugs so close, she couldn't bring herself to do it. She told herself it had nothing to do with the magic that had transpired between them.

But it was a bold-faced lie.

The thought of the precious hours she'd spent cocooned in his arms sent a rolling wave of pain through her center. Rachael had promised herself that after Michael died she would never put her heart on the line again. Giving that much only to risk having it taken away by fate was simply too much to bear.

She hadn't counted on Bo Ruskin coming into her life and throwing her carefully laid plans into turmoil. He was kind and caring with a character as firm and solid as stone. He was the kind of man a woman could fall in love with.

The truth shattered her.

She'd fallen in love with him.

The realization struck her with all the violence of the lightning bolts dancing on the horizon. The thought of love frightened her more than the prospect of facing off with Viktor Karas. How in the name of God could she have let that happen? How could she love the man who'd killed her husband?

But deep inside Rachael knew Bo Ruskin would never do such a thing— unless he had no choice. As painful as his words had been, she knew he wasn't lying about Michael.

I shot and killed him because he was working for Karas.

The enormity of those words crushed her. With sorrow. Grief. Regret. A terrible sense of betrayal. And rage.

Not all of that fury was focused on Bo. She was also angry with Sean Cutter for not trusting her. But mostly, she was angry with Michael. Why hadn't he come to her if he were being threatened?

She couldn't change the past. All she could do now was deal with what had been thrown at her and make things right as best she could. The only way to do that was to bring a vicious criminal to justice and end his violent reign once and for all.

Surprisingly, she wasn't unduly concerned for her own safety. Rachael trusted her skills and her instincts. Her willingness to jump into the fray was one of the things that had made her such a good agent, and so valuable to Sean Cutter. Some of her counterparts thought she was courageous. Some thought her a fool. Some had even accused her of having a death wish.

The truth of the matter was her current mindset was a combination of all three of those things.

A couple of miles from the homestead, the creek bed forked and became rocky. Having memorized the map before leaving, Rachael took the left fork and rode the horse up the steep bank and out of the rocks. If her memory served her, the cave was less than a mile ahead, where the creek made a hard curve to the south.

Stopping the horse, she eased her cell phone from its clip and flipped it open. She hit a series of buttons to activate the GPS chip inside, then dialed the number from which Karas had called her earlier. The kingpin picked up on the second ring.

"Ah, Ms. Armitage, what a pleasant surprise," he said in a cultured voice.

"Where's Cutter?"

"He's, shall we say, resting. He had a tough night."

A swirl of horror went through her at the thought of all the things that could have happened to Cutter, but she shoved her emotions aside and went with her instincts. "I'm tired of playing games with you, Karas. Put Cutter on the line and then you and I can talk about making a trade."

"Even if I had Cutter in my possession, I'm afraid there are very few things on this earth that would constitute an equal trade."

"You'll trade for what I have in mind. Now, put him on the phone."

A full minute passed before rustling sounded on the other end. "Armitage, damn it, what the hell are you doing?"

Relief swept through her at the sound of Cutter's voice. But he sounded as if he were under severe stress. "I'm going to save your life," she said.

"Put Ruskin on the—"

His sentence was interrupted abruptly by a groan. The snap of electricity. "Cutter?"

No answer.

Rachael closed her eyes, took several deep breaths to keep her emotions in check. They were torturing him. Bastards. She gripped the cell phone. "Cutter?"

More rustling, then Karas's voice returned. "Are you ready to negotiate?" he asked.

"I'm willing to make a trade." She closed her eyes tightly. "Your son's remains for the safe return of Sean Cutter."

Karas laughed. "You're in no position to make demands."

"If you want your son's remains, I suggest you shut your mouth and listen."

The silence that followed sent goose-flesh down her arms. "If I were you, I'd be very careful about what I say," he said in a dangerous tone.

"I'm not afraid of you," she spat. "I've never been afraid of you. I think you're pathetic. Your son was pathetic."

She could practically feel the fury coming through the line. She knew better than to taunt him; Viktor Karas was a brutal man and more than capable of making good on any threat. But Rachael knew it was the only way to manipulate a man who himself was a master manipulator.

"Your courage borders on foolhardiness," he said after a moment.

"It's not the first time I've been accused of that."

"Many of the people at your organization think you have a death wish."

"Maybe you think you can oblige."

Another laugh, only this time, it was an ugly, dangerous sound. "What trap have you set for me, Ms. Armitage?"

"All I want is Cutter."

"How is it that you have possession of my son's remains?"

"Not in my possession, but I know where his body is. It's unguarded. You give me Cutter, I give you the location."

Rachael let the silence work for a moment, knowing she had his undivided attention. Then she said, "I have GPS coordinates for you." She rattled off the coordinates of the caves Bo had told her about. "Bring Cutter. In a chopper. If I don't see him, the trade is off and you will never bring your son home."

She could hear the click of laptop keys in the background. The beep of a laptop computer. And she knew he was entering her GPS coordinates to locate her position.

"What's to stop me from killing both of you?" he asked.

"I'm well-armed, so don't try anything stupid."

"You really are a foolhardy bitch," he said mildly.

"And you want your son back."

A guttural scream sounded in the background. Rachael closed her eyes and tried not to think about what they were doing to Cutter.

"If you want me, come get me," she said and disconnected.

Chapter Fourteen

Bo pushed the horse to the limit of his endurance once he reached the open plain. It would have been safer to take the trail that ran along the dry creek bed. But Rachael had at least an hour head start on him. He had to reach her before she did something irrevocable.

He knew she'd already hatched some half-baked plan. That the plan was already in motion. The best he could hope for was that he would get there in time to save her life.

He wanted to be angry with her for acting so recklessly. She couldn't bring down Viktor Karas with a few explosives and a plan, no matter how brilliant. She might be a good agent, but she wasn't invincible.

But Bo wasn't angry with her in spite of what she'd done to him. She'd been through hell in the last two years. First she'd lost her husband, then found herself betrayed by the agency she'd devoted her life to.

Only then did he realize he wasn't going after her because she was a fellow agent. He wasn't trying to save her life because he'd been assigned to do so. He was risking his life to save hers because he loved her.

He couldn't believe he'd fallen for the one woman who was destined to hate him. The woman whose husband he'd shot and killed. The woman he'd lied to for two years. The woman whose world he'd shattered with a truth she should have been told a long time ago.

Leaning forward in the saddle, he urged the horse faster. The animal's back curved beneath him. Its hooves pounded the dry earth. Bo moved with the horse as if he were an extension of the animal itself. It was a dangerous pace on unfamiliar ground and in the middle of the night. Especially with a storm building to the west and desperation following him with every step. But if Bo wanted to reach

Rachael before Viktor Karas, he was going to have to take the risk.

Setting his hand against the rifle sheath at the rear of the saddle, he prayed he had the courage to use it when the time came.

IT TOOK RACHAEL ten minutes to reach the bend in the creek where Bo had said the caves were. Cliffs rose fifty feet on either side of the gully just past the curve. Even in the darkness, she could see the dark impressions where floodwaters had cut into the western side.

Dismounting, she tied the horse to a squatty pinion pine and threw the saddle-bag over her shoulder. Storm clouds moved swiftly past a three quarter moon. Shadows ebbed and flowed around her as she started up the steep wall of sandstone. It took her another ten minutes to find the cave.

The explosives are inside a watertight ammunition box beneath about a foot of sandy soil.

Bo's words echoed in her head as she turned on the flashlight and swept the beam along the sandstone walls. She'd considered the possibility that she wouldn't be able to find the explosives. But Rachael had to take the chance. She had to believe she would find them before Karas's chopper arrived.

Still, uncertainty swirled inside her as she stepped into the black expanse of the cave. It was twelve feet wide; the top rose only about six feet. The flashlight beam revealed it was a shallow cave, only about twenty feet deep.

She tried not to think about what she'd done to Bo as she swept the beam along the sandy floor, but the image of him filled her mind. The way he'd looked at her when she'd injected him. The way he'd pleaded for her not to go. The warmth and strength of his arms when he'd held her...

"I'm sorry, Bo," she whispered into the darkness.

Minutes ticked by as she searched the floor of the cave. Doubt began to plague her. Had she found the right cave? Were there really explosives buried here? Had Karas already found them? Could she really pull this off by herself?

Sweat broke out on her back as she searched the floor a second time. She went inch by inch, looking desperately for loose sand or a stone that had been recently moved. But she found nothing.

All the while she listened for the sound of rotor blades. If Karas arrived before she was ready, his men would storm the cave. She'd take out as many as she could, but her ammo was limited. Eventually, she would run out and they would overwhelm her. In the end, both she and Cutter would face gruesome deaths.

Her rapid breaths echoed off the cave walls as she began a third sweep. Desperate, she shone the light along the walls. Her heart lurched when she spotted the slight indentation at the very back of the cave where the ceiling was only a few feet high.

Dropping to her hands and knees, holding the light with one hand, she crawled toward the indentation. Relief swamped her when she spotted the disturbed earth. Propping the flashlight on a rock, she began digging with her hands. A few inches down, her fingers brushed against something steel. More digging revealed the steel ammo box. Wrestling the box from its sandy nest, she dragged it to the center of the cave for a better look.

The box was about two feet square and heavy. A shiny new padlock guarded the hasp. For an instant she considered shooting it off, but knew that with the box filled with explosives she would risk blowing it—and herself—to smithereens.

Pressed for time, she looked around wildly for something with which to break the padlock. Several pieces of driftwood lay in a pile at the mouth of the cave. But wood wasn't strong enough to break the steel lock. Noticing a large rock a few feet away, Rachael picked it up, gripped it tightly and brought it down as hard as she could on the lock. She hit the lock again and again, but did nothing more than dent the steel box. Sweating with nerves and physical effort, she realized she was going to have to take a chance and shoot off the lock.

She dragged the box to the mouth of the cave. Listening for the approach of a chopper, she drew her pistol. She positioned the padlock so the bullet would not penetrate the ammo box and fired a single shot. The padlock exploded on impact. The retort echoed through the canyon as she knelt and opened the box.

Bo had been cautious, wrapping each explosive in heavy canvas. Carefully, Rachael began unwrapping the cache. There were four grenades. A small supply of C-4 explosive. Fifty-caliber bullets—which were too large for her weapon. A remote control device. A small coil of wire. A switch. And a small submachine gun with an extra clip. Not the preferred weapon for bringing down a chopper, but a lucky shot just might do the trick.

He'd also included a gas mask with a ventilator, which could be used in case chemical or biological weapons were released into the air.

"You can take the man out of the agency, but you can't take the agent out of the man," she whispered.

Standing, Rachael checked her cell phone. The GPS chip in the phone was turned on. That meant Karas would be able to pinpoint her location. Kneeling, she removed two of the grenades and tucked them into the pockets of her coat. Next, she picked up the submachine gun and checked the large banana clip. Full. She shoved the extra banana clip into the waistband of her jeans. Her own pistol was nestled against her in a sleek leather shoulder holster.

There was one place nearby where the land was level and open enough to accommodate a chopper. She couldn't be sure, but she was betting Karas would have his pilot land there. If he did, she would be able to hear them coming. Kneeling, she picked up the two remaining grenades along with the small roll of wire, the remote control device and the switch. Using the flashlight, she quickly improvised an explosive she could detonate remotely. Her hands were shaking so badly she could barely manage the wires, but the MIDNIGHT Agency trained their agents well and in all sorts of situations. The dark, the fear, and the pressure to move quickly did not affect her ability.

When the device was complete, she wrapped the improvised explosive in canvas and stood. She was on her way to the mouth of the cave when the sound of a bullet being chambered stopped her dead in her tracks.

Chapter Fifteen

The cottonwood trees that grew in profusion near the cave had just come into view when the skies opened up. Rain and small hail fell in sheets as Bo entered the tree line. Twenty yards in, he spotted Rachael's horse.

"Easy, boy," he whispered as he approached.

Dismounting, he tied his horse next to Rachael's and looked around. The land surrounding the cave was the perfect place for an ambush. Rachael had ascertained that immediately upon seeing the map. He wondered if she'd found the cave. If she'd gotten to the explosives.

He wondered if Viktor Karas had already arrived....

His stomach clenched at the thought. Even though he was soaked to the skin, sweat squeezed from his pores when he set his hand against the rifle sheath.

It was too risky to use a flashlight, so Bo started into the darkness without it. He listened for the approach of a chopper over the din of rain as he wove through the cottonwood trees, but the downpour made it impossible to hear.

He moved into the sandy ravine with the silence of a nocturnal predator. Cliffs rose out of the dry creek bed on either side. Above, lightning split the night sky. Rain and wind pelted him, but he barely felt the cold. All he could think of was reaching the cave, finding the explosives intact and praying he wasn't too late.

He was twenty yards from the mouth of the cave when he spotted movement. Two figures standing near the low growing brush near the cave's entrance, one of which was unmistakably female.

Rachael, he thought, and his heart went wild in his chest. Ducking, Bo took cover behind a jut of sandstone. Simultaneously, his hand went to the pistol at his hip. But it wasn't the steady hand of the expert marksman he'd once been, but the shaky hand of a man who had way too much at stake to make a mistake.

Squinting through the pouring rain, he tried to make out what the figures were doing. That was when he spotted the third figure. Male. Bound. Judging from his posture, possibly injured. *Cutter,* he thought. Bo was pretty sure the man with the sawed-off shotgun was one of Karas's thugs, a Russian national—and known assassin—by the name of Ivan Petrov. He couldn't be sure, but the man near Rachel could have been Viktor Karas himself.

The last Bo had heard, the kingpin had been in Moscow. How had he gotten to the States so quickly and without alerting the MIDNIGHT Agency? And why would he risk capture when he had hundreds of mindless goons to do his bidding for him?

But Bo knew the answer to the latter question. The only time Viktor Karas made a personal appearance was when he wanted to make a point. This wasn't business as usual. This was personal. Karas wanted revenge for his son's death. He wanted to save face and prove once again his penchant for brutality. In order to accomplish that, he had to kill the one person responsible.

Rachael.

Sliding to a sitting position, Bo leaned against the rock and wiped rain from his face. He glanced at the rifle, willed himself to pick it up and take aim. But the familiar fear sweat broke out all over his body. His hands began to shake.

"Come on, damn it, you can do this!" he whispered.

But there was desperation in his voice. Panic gripped him so hard he could barely speak, barely draw a breath. Rachael's fate lay squarely in his hands.

The only question that remained was whether or not he was going to be able to save her or if the fear that had him in its clutches for two years would render him as useless as he felt.

RACHAEL STARED AT the man holding the deadly looking pistol at her chest and silently berated herself for not being more careful. He was young and as clean cut as a school boy. But Rachael knew looks could be deceiving. She was staring at none other than Ivan Petrov aka Ivan the Terrible.

A young assassin who'd murdered more than twenty-five people during the short span of his career. He was Viktor Karas's right-hand man. A man with a taste for killing and the will to climb to the top of Karas's illicit chain of command.

"Ivan Petrov." Dropping the last of the explosives she'd taken from the ammo box to the ground, she stepped toward him, praying he wouldn't spot them.

"And you are the illustrious Rachael Armitage." Amusement danced in his expression as his eyes swept over her. "I've heard you were stunning. The photographs do not do you justice."

"Forgive me if I'm not flattered."

"No offense taken." But his smile cooled. "Drop the gun. Put your hands up. Or I'll put a hole in that pretty body of yours."

Knowing he had her cold, she reached for the pistol. For an instant, she considered taking a wild shot. But the appearance of a second man out of the shadows stopped her. He was taller. Dressed in a flight suit and armed with a small submachine gun. The pilot, she realized.

With the speed of a striking snake,

Petrov grabbed her hand and yanked her toward him hard enough to make her stumble.

"Where's Cutter?" she asked.

A cold smile twisted Petrov's mouth. "We've been taking good care of your precious Cutter."

"Where is he, you son of a bitch?"

The smile turned icy. "They say you are a woman of fire and ice. We'll see how much fire you have inside you when we get you back to Moscow."

"I'm not going anywhere with you."

Her heart pounded like fists against her ribs. She couldn't believe she'd screwed up so badly. It was the first rule of the game. Never let your emotions dictate your actions. Rachael had done just that. And now she would probably pay with her life. Worse, she knew Cutter would, too.

But Viktor Karas never just killed, especially when he had a point to make. Both she and Sean Cutter would die long and slow deaths....

Movement in her peripheral vision interrupted her dark thoughts. She glanced toward the bushes at the edge of the clearing to see none other than Viktor Karas step out of the shadows.

"At last we meet."

The kingpin's cultured voice struck her like a slap. The cold reality of just how dire the situation had become struck her just as hard. For the first time in her career, she was frozen with fear. She wasn't going to get out of this alive. In the back of her mind she wondered if Bo had come after her. If he would find the explosives or if the drug had rendered him unable to follow...

"You'll never make it out of the country," she said.

Karas swept his arm in a 360-degree circle. "And who's going to stop me?"

"People at the agency know you're here."

"The agency has been crushed." He approached her, his expensive wingtips crunching through sand and stone. He wore a custom suit and expensive trench coat. His appearance was incongruous with their surroundings.

He looked at her as if she were some prized trophy animal whose head he wanted mounted on his wall. "I've knocked out their computers. Most of their communication." His mouth curved. "And let's suffice it to say I've cut off the head of the agency."

"Where's Cutter?" she repeated.

Never taking his eyes from hers, Karas snapped his fingers. As if on cue, another man shoved Sean Cutter out of the brush. Rachael caught a glimpse of a bruised face. A bloodstain on his shirt. Terrible knowledge in his eyes. His hands were bound behind his back. She wondered how many of his injuries had been sustained in the blast—and how many had been inflicted by these men.

A shove from behind sent Cutter sprawling. He landed facedown on his belly a yard from her feet.

"Cutter," she heard herself say.

"Ah, yes, the legendary Sean Cutter, untouchable head of the MIDNIGHT Agency." Karas set his foot on Cutter's back and ground his heel into his spine. "Not so untouchable now, are you, Mr. Cutter?"

Raising his head, Cutter spat mud and uttered a vile phrase.

Petrov lunged forward and landed a

kick in Cutter's face, then leveled his pistol at the back of his head. "Let me kill him now."

Karas snarled something in Russian, and Petrov lowered the pistol. Forgetting the men with guns, Rachael rushed to Cutter and dropped to her knees beside him. "How badly are you hurt?"

"Not so bad that I can't give you a dressing down for getting yourself into this situation," he growled.

Rachael squeezed her eyes closed at the reprimand. She couldn't believe the situation had boiled down to this moment. That there was a very good chance Viktor Karas would kill them both and get away with their murders.

"I'm sorry." She wrapped her hand around Cutter's arm and helped him turn over and sit up. "Easy," she said.

The cold steel of a gun rapped against the back of her head. "Leave him," said Ivan Petrov.

Before rising, Rachael leaned close to Cutter and whispered, "Ruskin is coming."

A minute nod from Cutter told her he'd heard her. She hoped her words gave him hope. At the moment, it was all she could do. Staring at the well-armed men surrounding them, hope seemed the one thing in very short supply.

Karas nodded at Petrov. "Bind her wrists and take them to the chopper. We're leaving."

Fear gripped Rachael. Boarding the chopper was the one thing she couldn't do. She wondered how far away the chopper was. If the walk to it would give Bo time to reach them.

She'd left him unconscious. Had he come to? Had he tracked her here? Even if he'd done both of those things, would he be able to do the one thing that for two years he hadn't?

"Get up."

A quiver ran the length of her body at the sound of Petrov's voice. Giving Cutter's arm a final squeeze, Rachael rose. She was aware of the pilot starting into the brush. Karas stood a few feet away. If she were going to make a move, it had to be now. She knew she wouldn't get away, but it might buy them some time.

Rachael bolted in the opposite direction of the men. A shout sounded behind her. Another shout in Russian to her left. She veered right and crashed through a stand of juniper. Her feet tangled in the branches, but she muscled through and somehow maintained her balance. Ahead, she saw darkness and rock and the cover of pinion pines.

Midway to the trees, a gunshot rent the air. She didn't think Karas would shoot her; he hadn't flown all the way from Moscow to Wyoming for such an unclimactic end. But Rachael had been wrong more often than not in the last few months and the fear that his was going to end badly never left her.

"Stop or I'll shoot Cutter, starting with his kneecaps!"

The words shocked her brain with a new and ugly fear. It was the only thing he could say that would stop her. At the edge of the trees, Rachael halted.

"Put your hands up."

Closing her eyes against the rush of regret, she did as she was told. She stood there, breathing hard, listening to the approach of footsteps.

"Turn around. Slowly."

Rachael turned.

The blow seemed to come out of nowhere. One moment she was turning to face her tormenter. The next she was on her knees, the side of her face aching.

"I'm going to enjoy killing you," Viktor Karas said.

Looking into the depths of his gaze and seeing the hatred, Rachael believed him.

The only question that remained was whether he would make good on his promise now, or wait until they reached his lair in Moscow.

Chapter Sixteen

Bo had never considered himself an emotional man. He'd certainly never considered himself impulsive. But when he saw Viktor Karas strike Rachael, the primal male fury to protect what was his exploded inside him. Perched on an outcropping of rock overlooking the dry creek bed below, there wasn't a damn thing he could do about it.

Except wait.

Even then, he faced even bigger problems. Not only did he have to line up for at least three shots under incredibly difficult conditions, but he was now also forced to face a fear that had twisted him into knots for two unbearable years. Could he conquer his fear and make the shots?

Two years ago he would have laughed at the absurdity of the situation. He'd been cocky, willing to try any shot, no matter how impossible. But after being forced to kill his best friend, Bo simply wasn't sure he could do it.

It was either make the shot or watch two people he cared for die. A man he'd called friend the entirety of his career. And a woman he loved more than life itself....

Even though he was soaked to the skin with rain and cold to the bone, sweat broke out all over his body when he looked down at the Remington. His hands shook as he pulled it from its sheath. He didn't have his sniper's tripod, but he could set up for the shot using the rock that surrounded him. His fingers were shaking so badly, it took two tries for him to mount the scope.

A hundred and fifty yards away, Karas helped Rachael to her feet. Bo steeled himself against the sight of her struggling as they bound her hands behind her back. Just beyond, Cutter sat on the ground, unable to do anything but watch. Both faced a terrible end if Bo couldn't pull this off.

Nausea seesawed in his gut when he lifted the rifle and set the long muzzle against the rock. Getting into the correct shooting position, Bo struggled to reach The Zone. The mental state where his focus was complete. Where nothing in the outside world mattered. A place where his only world consisted of what he saw through the scope. His target was not a person, but an objective that had to be reached.

Tonight, The Zone eluded him.

Wiping rain and sweat from his face, Bo put his eye to the scope and tried to focus. He would have to make two successive shots. Karas first, then Petrov. He adjusted the scope, nudged the muzzle right. The crosshairs settled on Karas. Center of chest. He didn't trust himself to make the headshot. The body made for a larger target. Tonight, with his hands shaking and his heart pounding like a piston, it was the best he could hope for.

His finger trembled against the trigger. He squinted, focused. He shifted left. Centered the crosshairs.

Holding his breath, he squeezed off the shot.

FOR A SPLIT SECOND Rachael thought the sound was a crack of thunder. She was in the process of getting to her feet when she noticed the bloom of red on Karas's trench coat. He was staring at her as if she'd just sucker punched him.

Shock vibrated through her when he grasped his abdomen and went to his knees.

Bo, she thought, and her legs nearly went weak with relief. But her relief was short-lived.

"Mr. Karas!"

She glanced beyond the fallen Karas to see Ivan Petrov sprinting toward them. The pilot had taken cover behind a fallen log. Beyond, Cutter stood, his eyes latched to the ridge behind her.

Instinct kicked in. Petrov was ten feet away, bringing his weapon up. But his focus was on Karas, not her, a mistake she could capitalize upon. Knowing this was her only chance, Rachael charged him. He swung the gun in her direction, but she landed a karate kick to his chest. He reeled backward, but maintained his grip on the weapon. With his finger already on the trigger, he sent a short burst of gunfire into the air.

Before he could regain his balance,

Rachael lunged and planted a second kick to his nose. As if in slow motion the weapon flew from his hands and landed several feet away. Vaguely she was aware of another gunshot from the ridge. Petrov reeled backward and landed squarely on his back.

She didn't wait to see what would happen next. Knowing she couldn't use the fallen weapon with her hands bound, she scrambled past Petrov.

"Cutter!" she screamed.

He was already running toward her. But his stride was awkward with his hands bound. "This way!" he shouted.

With Cutter at her side, she ran as fast as she could toward the closest cover, a line of pinion trees.

A volley of shots rang out as they reached the trees. But there was no time to look back. Rachael ran blindly through the darkness and rain, silently praying they were able to maintain their footing.

Past the trees, the ground dropped away. She stumbled over rocks the size of a basketballs. Next to her, Cutter went down, landing hard on his stomach.

"Go!" he shouted. "Leave me."

She darted to him. "Get up!"

"I'm hit," he ground out.

For the first time she noticed blood on his left thigh. "I'm not leaving you."

"I gave you a direct order, damn it."

"Shut up and run," she exhorted between clenched teeth.

"Stop or I'll shoot you both in the back." The words were quickly followed up by another burst of gunfire. "Stop!"

She envisioned bullets tearing through her spine. Beside her, Cutter struggled to his feet. She could hear someone breaking through brush behind them. Too fast. Too close.

"Run, damn it!" Cutter whispered.

She glanced at him. Shock vibrated through her when she saw blood coming through his coat. It looked black in the darkness. She couldn't see much, but enough for her to know it wasn't from some minor scratch. Cutter had been shot a second time.

"Cutter, my God..."

"Get your hands up!"

Rachael turned to see Ivan Petrov approach. He was twenty feet away. Blood dripped from his nose. His face was a mask of unconcealed fury, the submachine gun leveled at her chest. "I should shoot you both where you stand," he said.

Rachael could hear herself breathing hard, a combination of physical exertion and raw panic. Beside her, Cutter was bent at the hip, obviously in pain. Blood glittered black in the dim moonlight.

Petrov reached them. His lips pulled back into a snarl. Raising the rifle, he brought the butt down hard on Cutter's back. The agency head went to his knees.

"Stop it!" Rachael shouted. "He's been shot."

Petrov ignored her. His attention seemed divided. Turning slightly, his gaze skimmed the ridge above them. "It appears your friend Ruskin has decided to make an appearance."

Rachael closed her eyes at the thought of Bo. She knew about his phobia and could only imagine how difficult it must have been for him to pick off Karas. She wondered if he would be able to do it again. Or if he'd use the explosives...

She looked at Petrov. "You're surrounded," she said. "Give it up."

Hatred gleamed in the young man's

eyes when he turned them on her. "I'll kill all of you before I do that."

"Then run," she offered. "Run to the border while you still have a chance to get away."

The smile he gave her sent a chill all the way to her bones. "I have a score to settle first."

"What score?"

For the first time his gaze faltered. "I owe it to Viktor to finish this. He was like a father to me."

A very twisted father, she thought. But Rachael didn't voice the sentiment. All she could do was stand mutely while the sociopath trained the gun on her heart.

They were standing on an outcropping of rock. On one side was the ridge where she hoped Bo was trying to get into position for another shot. But she knew the distance would be difficult even in the best of conditions. The heavy rain and darkness would make a long-distance shot nearly impossible. Plus there was wind and a line of trees and darkness to obscure his vision.

She glanced over her shoulder. Opposite the rise, the earth sloped steeply downward toward the dry creek bed. In the darkness she couldn't tell how far the slope went, but if worse came to worse, she and Cutter could brave the cliff and hope the fall didn't kill them.

The pilot approached from out of the trees, a pistol in his hand. "Mr. Petrov, perhaps we should leave," he said.

Petrov nodded, but his eyes kept going to the ridge. He knew Bo was up there. Knew they were in the line of fire. He looked at Rachael, then at the pilot.

"We kill them here." He motioned toward her and Cutter. "Put them facedown on the ground. I'll take care of the rest."

Nodding, the pilot started toward her.

"Please don't do this," she said and stepped toward Petrov.

The Russian leveled his weapon on her chest. "Don't get any closer."

His words were punctuated by a low rumble of thunder. But Rachael barely heard it over the wild beat of her heart. She couldn't believe she and Cutter were probably going to be shot execution-style before Bo could get into position for another shot. And that their killers would probably get away with murder.

Thunder rumbled incessantly and so hard the ground beneath her feet seemed to tremble. It was as if the nucleus of the storm was upon them and the earth shook with fear.

Every nerve in her body jerked taut when the pilot grasped the back of her collar and tried to force her to the ground. She resisted. Blood roared in her ears now, keeping perfect time with the storm. She could no longer tell if she was trembling or if the earth was shaking.

Another clap of thunder shook the ground. Rachael looked up to see an orange plume rise forty feet into the air on the near horizon beyond the trees. At first she thought lightning had struck. Then she remembered the explosives…and Bo.

Spinning toward the explosion, Petrov shouted something in Russian to the pilot. Knowing she wouldn't have another opportunity, Rachael jerked from the pilot's grasp and spun. He raised his weapon. She lashed out with her foot, catching him in the center of his chest. He reeled backward.

Behind him, she saw Cutter struggle to his feet. Twenty feet away Petrov fired a shot. Cutter scrambled toward the ledge. Vaguely, Rachael heard something crashing through brush. In her peripheral vision, she saw something large and dark enter the clearing. *Bo,* she thought, just as another gunshot split the air.

Bo Ruskin was astride the Appaloosa and traveling at a dangerous speed. He held a rifle in one hand, a pistol in the other. He gripped the leather reins between his teeth. Petrov fired a wild shot, then ran toward cover.

Then the horse was beside her. She had a split second to act and grabbed his outstretched hand. His strength and the momentum of the horse's movement helped her to swing onto the saddle behind him.

"Lean against me!" he shouted, knowing her hands were bound.

The horse spun on a dime. Bo fired off four shots in quick succession in the general direction of Petrov, but the Russian was nowhere in sight.

"Cutter!" she shouted. "There! He's been shot!"

Bo spurred the horse. The animal sprinted toward Cutter. Two more shots rang out. Rachael turned her head to see Karas standing within the trees, the rifle leveled on them. "Bo!"

Bo raised the pistol, but the horse was moving too fast, the ride too violent for him to aim. But he fired blindly. A muzzle flash came from within the line of trees and she knew Petrov was not yet down.

"Cutter!" Bo shouted. "The ravine! Jump!"

Cutter didn't need to be told twice. He stumbled awkwardly toward the edge where the water had cut a deep gorge and disappeared over the edge.

Rachael's mind barely had time to process that when she realized Bo was going to take the horse over the edge as well.

"Bo!" she screamed.

And the horse leapt into space.

Chapter Seventeen

The horse landed on its haunches and slid twenty feet in deep sand before regaining its balance. Rachael closed her eyes and leaned hard against Bo.

The ride down the steep slope was as wild as any roller coaster. As a child Rachael had always been a fan of roller coasters. As an adult, she'd set her sights on a different kind of thrill. She hadn't bargained for riding blind into what could turn out to be a suicide rescue.

The horse struggled to maintain its footing as it slid on its haunches down the slope at a dangerous speed. Mud and small debris flew up from its hooves as the animal muscled through brush and hurtled roots and branches.

All Rachael could do was pray she didn't fall off.

The descent seemed to take forever. She caught glimpses of trees and flashes of lightning. In the back of her mind she wondered about Cutter. She wondered if the men above them had night-vision equipment and would continue shooting.

The horse reached the base of the ravine and skidded to an abrupt halt. She felt Bo relax, then he reached down and patted the trembling animal's shoulder.

"Easy, boy," he murmured. "Good boy."

He dismounted, then reached for her. "Are you all right?"

Rachael was no stranger to high adrenaline. But every muscle in her body quivered as he eased her to the ground. "I'm not sure yet."

Pulling a knife from his belt, he turned her and slashed the nylon binding her wrists. For a moment she couldn't find her voice. Then she looked into his eyes. "You blew up the chopper?"

"I knew those explosives would come in handy one day."

She didn't intend to reach for him. But at the moment she needed to feel his arms around her more than she needed to take her next breath. Putting her arms around his shoulders, she closed her eyes against the rush of pleasure when he put his arms around her and held her tight.

"It's all right," he said. "We're going to be okay."

"You saved our lives."

"Yeah, well, it ain't over yet." Gently, he eased her to arm's length.

The hairs at her nape prickled as she looked up the steep ravine. Seeing the impossibly rugged terrain, she almost couldn't believe the horse had taken them safely down without so much as a misstep.

"We need to find Cutter." Patting the horse's shoulder, he walked the animal to a low growing tree and tied it. "I have a feeling Karas isn't finished yet."

"Cutter has been shot," she said. "Twice, I think."

Even in the dim light she saw him grimace. "We need to find him and fast." He motioned left. "Let's fan out. Try not to make any noise. They may just be crazy enough to follow us."

Giving her a last look, he disappeared into the darkness.

She was still shaking when she started along the foot of the cliff. The ride into the ravine had been so wild she couldn't tell where they'd landed in relation to where Cutter had gone over the edge.

"Cutter?" she whispered into the darkness. "Cutter?"

The sound of a twig breaking off to her left sent her heart slamming against her ribs. Rachael spun.

And found herself looking at a deadly pistol and the bloodied face of Viktor Karas.

"WE MEET AGAIN, Ms. Armitage."

Her gaze flicked past him. In an instant her mind scrolled through a dozen different scenarios. He was outnumbered. Obviously injured. But she knew an injured predator was the most dangerous.

"If you scream I'll put a bullet between your eyes."

"You're going to do that anyway."

"I want my son's remains. I'm willing to wait for the rest."

She stared at him. A two-inch cut on his temple spread blood down the right side of his face. Lower, more blood marred the front of his trench coat.

"You've been shot," she said.

"Twice, actually. But the Kevlar vest did its job." A tremor went through her when he raised the gun a fraction of an inch and pointed it at her forehead. "Now where are my son's remains?"

She saw the tension go through his arm. Even in the semidarkness, she saw his finger move on the trigger. Her only thought was that she was going to die. That she would never see Bo again. She would never get the chance to tell him she loved him.

"Don't," she heard herself say.

The smile that split his face looked macabre in the semidarkness. "Did my son beg for his life?"

"Your son tried to kill me. It was self-defense."

"Where are his remains?" he repeated.

"He was buried in Washington, D.C." It was a lie; Rachael had no idea where the government had buried his son. "Cherry Hill Cemetery, near Dulles Airport."

Hatred glittered diamond sharp in the depths of his eyes. "Get on your knees."

Rachael knew the moment she acquiesced, he would execute her. "Please."

"Do it."

Taking her time, she got down on both knees.

"Beg for your life," he said.

She looked at him, wondering in some small corner of her mind if he'd lost touch with reality. If the pressure of his lifestyle had finally sent him around the bend. "I don't know what you want me to say."

His lips pulled back in a snarl. "I said beg, bitch. Figure it out."

Her heart was beating so hard she could barely hear him. "Please don't kill—"

A gunshot fractured the night.

From his position behind a jut of granite ten yards away, Bo saw Rachael's body jolt, and his heart stopped dead in his chest. All he could think was that Karas had fired simultaneously. That she would die before he got to her side. That he would never hold her again. Or look into her eyes and see all the things that were good and right in the world.

Only then did it strike him that somehow he'd lined up for a shot and taken it. He'd hit Karas with the first shot, and it had been fatal. The fear that had gripped him for so many months fled the instant he'd known it was either take the shot—or lose Rachael forever.

None of that mattered now. All he cared about was Rachael. Praying he hadn't taken the shot too late, he shoved the pistol into the waistband of his jeans and started toward her at a dead run.

For a terrible moment, Rachael thought Karas had shot her. Then she realized she hadn't felt the impact. That the shot had come from somewhere else.

Across from her Viktor Karas went to his knees. His gaze locked on hers. He hovered there for several interminable seconds. He tried to raise the pistol, but he wasn't strong enough. She heard a rush of breath from his lungs, then he fell forward and lay still.

Rachael tried to get to her feet, but her legs were shaking so violently she couldn't manage. She jolted when strong hands landed on her shoulders.

"Easy." Bo's voice penetrated the after-shocks of fear. "I've got you."

"Is he…?" She couldn't finish the sentence. Couldn't speak.

"He's gone." Gently, he helped her to her feet. "It's over."

Relief made her legs go weak all over again. "Cutter?"

"Sheriff's office is sending a chopper compliments of the agency. If they can get him to a trauma center quickly, I think he's going to be okay." Turning her to face him, he looked into her eyes, his gaze dark with concern. "I'm not so sure about you."

Only then did she realize she was crying. Her entire body trembled. "I'm sorry," she said.

"You're entitled." Bending slightly, he swept her into his arms. "You've been through a lot."

"You saved my life twice tonight."

"You didn't make it easy." He smiled down at her. "But then nothing worth anything ever is."

Epilogue

Rachael walked toward Sean Cutter's makeshift office and tried not to think about what would transpire once she entered. She should have been prepared; after all, she'd known this final meeting was inevitable after the way things had played out with Viktor Karas and Ivan Petrov. But then one could never prepare for the end of a career they loved.

Around her, painting contractors rolled institutional gray paint onto new Sheetrock. Polyurethane sheeting covered the open spaces where new walls would replace the ones that had been damaged in the bombing. The agency had wasted no time in the rebuilding effort. If only rebuilding her life would be so simple.

Her heart beat hard and fast in her chest when she rapped on the door. Cutter's curt voice sounded from inside, telling her to enter. Taking a deep, calming breath Rachael turned the knob and pushed open the door.

Sean Cutter sat behind a beat-up metal desk she sorely hoped was temporary. He wore a nicely cut suit, but the left sleeve hung useless at his side. His arm was in a sling, probably from the bullet wound he'd sustained three days ago in that Wyoming creek bed. He was lucky to be alive. All three of them were.

Across from him, Bo Ruskin leaned back in a metal folding chair. He was wearing a black felt cowboy hat, high-end western boots and jeans that reminded her of the night she'd spent in his arms. A memory that would be with her the rest of her life.

"Have a seat," Cutter began.

She took the chair next to Bo. She could feel his eyes on her, but she couldn't look at him. She wasn't sure how she would react or what she would feel. She didn't know how to be in love. She sure as hell didn't know how to say goodbye. To the man she loved—and the career she'd devoted her entire adult life to building.

Gathering her resolve, she focused her attention on Cutter, met his gaze levelly. "How are you feeling?"

"Shoulder hurts like hell, but I'm going to be okay. I start physical therapy next week."

"Good." She nodded with ridiculous enthusiasm.

A tense silence sounded for the span of several heartbeats, then Cutter opened the file on his desk and gave her a pointed look. "I could spend the next couple of hours dressing you down for the way you handled the Karas situation during your mandatory time off."

Here it comes, she thought.

"But I won't."

Surprise rippled through her, but it was tempered by anxiety. Because her hands wanted to shake, Rachael set them on her thighs and resisted the urge to wipe the sweat from her palms. "I appreciate that."

Cutter motioned at Ruskin. "Bo said you were instrumental in bringing this to an end, Rachael."

Finally, she risked a look at Bo. His eyes

were already on her, probing as if he were trying to figure out what she was thinking, what she was feeling. She wasn't even sure herself.

"If it hadn't been for Ms. Armitage," Bo said, "Viktor Karas would have blindsided us, more than likely killing everyone at my ranch. He would have taken me and Ms. Armitage hostage and then fled the border into Canada and ultimately to Moscow."

It was the last thing she'd expected Bo to say. Last she'd heard, he'd called her reckless and accused her of having a death wish.

"That's still not to say you disregarded a few direct orders," Cutter added.

"Just a few," she said dryly.

"But I'm a firm believer in that courage and heroism should be rewarded." He grimaced. "I'm only sorry I didn't support you in your endeavors to bring down this dangerous criminal early on. Frankly, I was worried about your safety. I was afraid you'd cross a line and get yourself hurt." He smiled. "Instead, it was me who got hurt. And I owe both of you thanks for saving my life."

Rachael didn't know what to say. Walking into Sean Cutter's office, she'd feared losing her job. Losing her identity. Most of all she'd feared losing the man she loved more than her own life.

Gathering her resolve, she met Cutter's stare head-on. "I know what I did was risky, Sean. But I believe in right and wrong. I still believe that good prevails over evil. I'm just glad that I could do my part to end Viktor Karas's reign of terror."

Cutter smiled. "In that case, I wanted to give you a heads up that I've got another assignment in mind for you. North Africa. Deep cover."

Rachael sat up straighter. Usually, she was champing at the bit and ready to go at the drop of a hat when it came to assignments. This time, however, she wasn't any of those things. All she could think of was that she wanted to take care of some unfinished business with the cowboy sitting next to her first.

The realization stunned her. For the first time in the course of her career, she wanted time off. Time to make things right with Bo.

"I'm afraid I can't accept the mission," she heard herself say.

The two men exchanged looks. Rachael could feel her heart beating hard and fast. Her palms slicking with sweat.

"Why not?"

"I'd like to take some time off," she blurted.

"Time off?"

"To take care of some unfinished business," she said. "In Wyoming."

"All right." But for the first time since she'd known him, Sean Cutter seemed at a loss. He looked down at the file in front of him. "You have some vacation coming."

"How much?"

"Three weeks."

"I'll take it all," she said.

"When?"

"Right now."

Cutter's eyes went from Rachael to Bo, then back to Rachael. "You got it."

"Thank you," she said.

Cutter rose. "Now if you'll excuse me, I'm going to go get a cup of coffee if I can find the coffeemaker in this mess."

Rachael watched him limp to the door

and quietly close it behind him. The silence that followed was deafening.

"Cutter's a good man," Bo said after a while.

Turning in her chair, she faced him, faced the very thing she'd feared most since setting eyes on him just one short week ago. "He's an astute man," she said.

Rachael swallowed hard when he rose to his full height. Her heart hammered against her breastbone when he reached for her and pulled her to his feet.

She looked into his eyes. Within the depths of his gaze, she saw respect. Admiration. Affection. She saw everything except the one thing she needed to see most.

"He asked me to come back to the agency," he said.

"Did you agree?"

He shook his head. "Not my game anymore." He smiled. "But it's yours. I want you to go for it. I want you to do what you want."

"I'm good at that, I guess." But suddenly she was terrified he was letting her go. He was giving her what she wanted. What he *thought* she wanted.

"It's not what I want," she blurted.

His dark eyebrows snapped together. "Come again?"

"I want to go back to the ranch with you. I want to learn to ride. I want to learn about Appaloosas. I want to spend the next three weeks getting to know you without having to worry about some madman trying to kill us."

Rachael was generally adept at speaking her mind and more than capable of keeping her composure while under pressure. When it came time to speak her heart, however, the words were tumbling out in disarray.

"I thought you wanted to get back to work," he said. "I wanted to give you the freedom to do that. I wanted to give you the time to do what you need to do before we...before I—"

"I've always believed in the old adage, 'If you love something set it free,'" she said.

He smiled. "If it's meant to be, it will come back."

"You gave me the chance to go," she whispered.

"I thought that was what you wanted."

"My priorities have shifted, Bo." She

closed her eyes briefly. "The only thing I want right now is some time with you."

Putting his hands on either side of her face, he searched her gaze. "I reckon that means this was meant to be."

"I reckon so," she said.

"You've been hanging out with too many cowboys."

"Probably. But I love this cowboy. I love everything about him. I want to hang out with him the rest of my life."

"You just made me the happiest cowboy in the world," he said, and lowered his mouth to hers.

Happily ever after is just the beginning....

Turn the page for a sneak preview of
DANCING ON SUNDAY AFTERNOONS
by
Linda Cardillo

Harlequin Everlasting—Every great love
has a story to tell.™
A brand-new line from Harlequin Books
launching this February!

Prologue

Giulia D'Orazio
1983

I had two husbands—Paolo and Salvatore.

Salvatore and I were married for thirty-two years. I still live in the house he bought for us; I still sleep in our bed. All around me are the signs of our life together. My bedroom window looks out over the garden he planted. In the middle of the city, he coaxed tomatoes, peppers, zucchini—even grapes for his wine—out of the ground. On weekends, he used to drive up to his cousin's farm in Waterbury and bring back manure. In the winter, he wrapped the peach tree and the fig tree with rags and black rubber hoses against the cold, his massive, coarse hands gentling those trees as if they were his fragile-skinned babies. My neighbor, Dominic Grazza, does that for me now. My boys have no time for the garden.

In the front of the house, Salvatore planted roses. The roses I take care of myself. They are giant, cream-colored, fragrant. In the afternoons, I like to sit out on the porch with my coffee, protected from the eyes of the neighborhood by that curtain of flowers.

Salvatore died in this house thirty-five years ago. In the last months, he lay on the sofa in the parlor so he could be in the middle of everything. Except for the two oldest boys, all the children were still at home and we ate together every evening. Salvatore could see the dining room table from the sofa, and he could hear everything that was said. "I'm not dead, yet," he told me. "I want to know what's going on."

When my first grandchild, Cara, was born, we brought her to him, and he held her on his chest, stroking her tiny head. Sometimes they fell asleep together.

Over on the radiator cover in the corner of the parlor is the portrait Salvatore and

I had taken on our twenty-fifth anniversary. This brooch I'm wearing today, with the diamonds—I'm wearing it in the photograph also—Salvatore gave it to me that day. Upstairs on my dresser is a jewelry box filled with necklaces and bracelets and earrings. All from Salvatore.

I am surrounded by the things Salvatore gave me, or did for me. But, God forgive me, as I lie alone now in my bed, it is Paolo I remember.

Paolo left me nothing. Nothing, that is, that my family, especially my sisters, thought had any value. No house. No diamonds. Not even a photograph.

But after he was gone, and I could catch my breath from the pain, I knew that I still had something. In the middle of the night, I sat alone and held them in my hands, reading the words over and over until I heard his voice in my head. I had Paolo's letters.

* * * * *

Be sure to look for
DANCING ON SUNDAY AFTERNOONS
available January 30, 2007.
And look, too, for our other Everlasting
title available,
FALL FROM GRACE by Kristi Gold.

FALL FROM GRACE
is a deeply emotional story
of what a long-term love really means.
As Jack and Anne Morgan discover,
marriage vows can be broken—
but they can be mended, too.
And the memories of their marriage have
an unexpected power to bring back
a love that never really left....

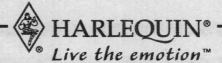

HARLEQUIN®
INTRIGUE®

BREATHTAKING ROMANTIC SUSPENSE

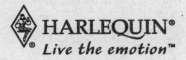

HARLEQUIN®
Presents

The world's bestselling romance series...
The series that brings you your favorite authors,
month after month:

Helen Bianchin...Emma Darcy
Lynne Graham...Penny Jordan
Miranda Lee...Sandra Marton
Anne Mather...Carole Mortimer
Susan Napier...Michelle Reid

and many more uniquely talented authors!

Wealthy, powerful, gorgeous men...
Women who have feelings just like your own...
The stories you love, set in exotic, glamorous locations...

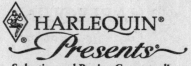

Seduction and Passion Guaranteed!

HARLEQUIN®

Super Romance®

...there's more to the story!

Superromance.
A *big* satisfying read about unforgettable
characters. Each month we offer *six* very different
stories that range from family drama to adventure
and mystery, from highly emotional stories to
romantic comedies—and much more! Stories
about people you'll believe in and care about.
Stories too compelling to put down....

Our authors are among today's *best* romance
writers. You'll find familiar names and talented
newcomers. Many of them are award winners—
and you'll see why!

If you want the biggest and best
in romance fiction, you'll get it
from Superromance!

Exciting, Emotional, Unexpected...

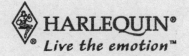

HARLEQUIN®
Live the emotion™